Walk

With

Big Foot

C. S. Clifford

First published in Great Britain 2017

ISBN: 9 780993 195792

Printed and bound in the UK

A catalogue record of this book is available from the British Library

Edited by Chloe S Chapman and Emma Batten

Cover by Anna E Howlett of Rosehart Studio

For the continued inspiration I receive from the children I teach.

To Honey

Best Wishes

CSC...

Prologue

Matt and James discovered a portal to another time and place at the start of their summer holidays, by chance, during their training to get fit for the approaching rugby season. While swimming underwater in the local river, Matt had found a cave at the base of a waterfall. The two boys eagerly explored the cavern and tunnel leading from it to a second waterfall. Running alongside was a narrow ledge which allowed them to pass through the deluge into a strange new world. This is their fifth adventure through the waterfall and into the unknown...

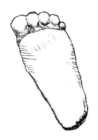

Chapter 1:
Time to Go

Matt walked up to the garden gate of James' house and was about to open it when his friend appeared at the front door.

"Perfect timing Matt, I thought I'd come and meet you early but it looks like you've beaten me to it."

"Yeah, I was feeling restless, thought it was about time we had a talk about the waterfall again."

"Well it's time. Let's wait until we get away from here though; make sure that nobody overhears us."

The two boys walked up the street side by side without saying another word. They turned left at the end and headed towards an open field full of slowly ripening wheat. Skirting the perimeter, they then entered a small wood before coming to the river that led to their biggest secret. They followed it for about a mile before coming to a graceful incline that heralded a series of gentle rolling hills. The river meandered around the bottom of several of them before ending at the waterfall which was their favourite place in all the world. Feeling a tingling sensation of anticipation, at what it concealed, they sat down on the river bank and stared at it.

"We've been back for four days now James, and already I'm getting restless."

"I know what you mean, each time we've travelled we've been away for three or four weeks. Every time we come back the period before we go through it again becomes less. It's almost like having a craving for chocolate or something. You've got to have it; in this case we've got to go."

"There's no doubt about going it's just a case of when."

"We could go right now, experience tells us that we don't need to take anything. The question is are you as ready to go as I am, and I already know the answer to that?"

Matt's face erupted into a huge grin.

"It's so hot already today that the water's going to seem very cold."

"When did something like that ever stop you from jumping in?" James laughed. "But, like last time, you are not going to be the one who goes in first."

James stood suddenly, taking Matt completely by surprise, he ran and launched himself into a swallow dive entering less than gracefully. Matt stood to follow but James had disappeared under before he reached the water. Even though he knew he could never overtake James he didn't shirk at the challenge; he dove and swam swiftly to the waterfall. A few feet from it, he took a deep breath and ducked under, swimming down to the base of it. Seeing the cave, he entered it and followed the twists and turns that led upwards into the heart of the hillside.

The route was second nature to him now and he soon emerged in the pool room. He was surprised that there was no sign of James but the tunnel that headed from their position led only to one place.

Leaving the pool he followed it, noticing the marks that James had originally made on the wall the first time they came here. He grinned at the memory before picking up the pace.

A moment or two later he burst out into a wide open cavern. Diffused light showered the space and danced on the walls as it found its way through a second waterfall whose thunderous roar blocked out all other sounds.

"What kept you?" James shouted above the din and grinning in an unusually smug way.

He stood by the ledge at the corner of the waterfall. There was no way that Matt could pass him without resorting to rugby tactics - both boy's favourite sport. James had tricked him and robbed him of his right to go first. Matt loved to go first, needed to go first, at everything he did, and to begin with he felt a mild sense of annoyance. Then he realised that James had just copied the sort of thing he would have done to take the leading role and he grinned knowingly.

James grinned again knowing that for a change he had the pole position. He indicated for Matt to follow and started to sidle along the ledge, again before Matt could even respond. The water cascaded down on his head and he closed his eyes until he had moved all the way through it. He opened and then wiped them, staring at the view ahead while he waited for Matt to join him. Matt appeared opening and rubbing his eyes.

"Wow! Look at that, have you ever seen such a large area of woodland?"

"Never, it's absolutely massive."

The boys had emerged from the waterfall halfway up a hillside that held a few scattered trees. From their position they were above the canopy of a vast forest and could see for miles in front of them. There was no end to the trees - no buildings, no settlements, just trees.

"Mmm, we seem to be a long way from anywhere and people," James pondered.

"The weight of the water as we passed through was a lot lighter this time, similar to the trip where we ended up in Scotland."

"I agree Matt, which means we haven't gone back in time very far."

"What's your best guess?"

"Twentieth century, maybe nineteenth."

"Well there aren't any clues around here to tell us, so let's go because it looks like we've a lot of ground to cover before we start getting any answers."

James clambered down the rocks at the side of the waterfall and then jumped down onto the earthy ground; Matt followed closely.

"Which way?" James asked allowing his friend to take his more accustomed role.

Matt strode off without answering and James fell in behind. It was always like this, the two friends were very different characters and yet their differences made them a formidable team. James was thoughtful and calm whilst Matt was headstrong and impulsive.

They knew each other like brothers and seldom argued despite their differences. Their common ground was a love for rugby and having adventurous natures. While seeking adventure used to get them into trouble both at school and home, when they went through the time portal they found that it was advantageous in solving problems in the past. This was the fifth time they had passed through looking for adventure and both were feeling the adrenaline rush and sense of anticipation.

"There's no sign of any path to follow and that could mean a problem in finding our way back here."

"The hill with the waterfall was the only hill I could see which means we only have to look for that when we go back."

"Impressive Matt, when did you start thinking about things ahead of the game?"

"We talked about this a bit before, that we felt that we were changing a bit."

"I think it's because of the length of time we are in each place and that we always seem to be adults."

"I agree; it's bound to rub off on us eventually."

"You know Matt, I had a horrible thought the other day - what if we changed to a woman."

"Trust you to think of something like that James. Hopefully that will never happen. "

"They would probably call you Mat-ilda," James said laughing.

"I don't know why you are laughing, you'd have to be called Jame-lia or something," Matt laughed back.

"Anyway it's not likely that we would be women."

"Why not?"

"It's just not."

They let the subject drop and continued their walk through the forest.

"The birds are in full voice James but I haven't seen any animals yet."

"I'm wondering what country we are in because I don't think we are in the UK."

"Where are we then?"

"I'm not sure, but I don't think there are any forests of this size in the UK."

"The trees are of mixed varieties."

"I've noticed that too which means we can probably rule out more northern countries like Scandinavia."

"So we would be looking at places with a large land mass then?"

"Yes I think so, but I don't think we are going to get any further clues until we reach some sort of civilisation."

"Changing the subject for a moment James but I think I see some sort of path or trail just ahead."

"Let's follow that for a while and see where it leads us."

The boys walked for another hour, following the trail and stopping at a small stream to quench their thirst, before Matt spotted something in a small clearing to his left.

"Look at this James, someone's been here, made a camp fire. Look at all the footprints here too."

"There's more than one set Matt, different sizes and different tread patterns."

"Well it's a positive sign, at least we know we are not alone out here."

The footprints led from the clearing onto the path they were following and after such a long period without anything to suggest they were heading the right way, the boys' moods were lifted a little. The relentless walking and the limited scenery continued and soon the light started to dim.

"It looks to me as if we are going to have to camp for the night. It's going to be pitch black in here soon and it could be dangerous to try and travel when we can't see where we are going," James said a little disappointedly. "I can't believe we have walked so far without seeing someone."

"I can't believe you are thinking of camping overnight. We've nothing with us and we have no idea what creatures live in these woods. Then we'll keep going, if we stick to the trail we should be alright."

James acquiesced suddenly, conceding that Matt might be right about wild creatures in these woods.

"Ok we keep on moving."

The light continued to fall and seeing anything beyond a few yards became impossible. The woods were dense and the canopy thick but every now and then a small gap allowed a silver shaft of moonlight to penetrate to the ground. The boys had lost all sense of time now and had no real idea how far they had travelled but they were tiring and the monotony was getting to them. Suddenly, a chilling howl broke the otherwise silence of the woods. It stopped them dead in their tracks, as it seemed to creep menacingly through the trees. They had heard this howl before many times in films and nature programs. There could be no mistake. It was the cry of a wolf.

"We've got to get out of here James and fast."

"Let's pick up the pace a bit."

"We should run or at least jog, wolves are pack animals and move fast."

"Ok let's jog; we can keep that up for longer."

For the next fifteen minutes they kept up a pace that was a little faster than a jog before Matt slowed and stopped.

"Can you see what I see ahead, or am I imaging it?

"If you mean an orange glow of the type that normally hovers over a town then I see it."

They started running again, this time faster than their previous pace, closer and closer to the orange glow before reaching the end of the trees and bursting out into a large clearing with four small log cabins. They slowed to a stop and stared whilst fighting to catch their breath.

Chapter 2:
Company

The cabins had been constructed in a rough circle and a large camp fire burned brightly at the centre of it. Several human shapes sat around and some kind of beast roasted on a spit above emitting smells that made their mouths water.

"Civilisation at last." James said and walked toward the fire.

He only managed two steps before one of them stood and pointed a rifle at them.

"Stay exactly where you are and identify yourself." A woman's voice carried the distance between them clearly.

"We're not here to harm you and we've walked a very long way to get here so there's no need for the rifle."

"I'll be the judge of that; who are you?"

"It's all right Sarah. Put the gun down and let me introduce you to the Courtney Brothers. These two are probably amongst the top ten trackers in the whole world. They are the ones I told you about when I went to Kenya."

The second female voice was calmer, more refined; definitely English and from a wealthy educated family, judging by the way she spoke.

"Surely you didn't walk all the way here; where are your horses?"

"We came by foot, it's the best way to get a feel for the local area."

"Well it's hardly local but I have to say I'm impressed. Tell me which one of you is Matthew and which is James?"

"I'm James and this is Matthew, although he would prefer it if you call him Matt."

The second woman pushed herself in front of Sarah and held out her hand in greeting.

"Nice to meet you fellows, I'm Dr Susan Blanchett."

She shook hands with each of them.

"This is Sarah, my assistant. Come to the fire and I'll introduce you to the other members of my group."

They took the remaining few steps forward and came face to face with three men.

"This is Carson Rogers, a local man who has appointed himself as the protector of Canada's greatest mythological creature. These two are yet another set of brothers, meet David and Wayne Johnson, they are local men hired to pander to my own, and the expeditions every need."

Formal handshaking commenced before the brothers rudely turned their backs on the new arrivals and sat back in their seats.

Carson remained standing and smiled warmly at them.

"I'm guessing that you're both hungry and thirsty after your hike. We have baked potatoes and fresh pork on the spit. There are some vegetables too. I will get Wayne to serve you whilst David can fetch a rather lovely claret I found in Paris on my last trip," Susan offered.

Both men scowled before getting up and following their instructions. Matt and James knew instantly that they had work to do to win the two of them over.

"You are very thoughtful madam, thank you," James said formally.

"Please forget the formality of titles and just call me Susan or Dr; whichever you prefer."

While they ate Susan gave them some details about the forthcoming expedition.

"Everything we need for a month long trek is here ready and waiting. There are two wagons behind your cabin, which is that one there by the way," she said pointing. They are filled to the brim with food and supplies of all sorts, including scientific equipment and weapons. I assumed that you would have your own rifles but I see no evidence of that. In point of fact you have travelled extremely light. Where are your bags?"

"You did say that you were taking care of the supplies so we didn't bother bringing anything. As far as rifles go, we are trackers not hunters." James answered.

Wayne and David both shook their heads in disgust and Wayne interrupted the conversation.

"Have you any idea how dangerous the wilds of Canada actually are, do you know what sort of animals roam these woods?"

"You mean bears, wild boar, wolves and things?" Matt answered trying to match Wayne's sarcasm.

"And don't forget the reason we are all here for - according to sightings these things are over eight feet tall."

"We didn't need rifles in Kenya for Rhinos, Lions, elephants, hippos and other big cats. Rather makes your creatures seem more like teddy bears in comparison doesn't it?" James added his own sarcasm.

"Our wild creatures may be smaller but they are equally dangerous," David countered.

"You might be right but we are not going to use rifles; it's not our way."

Carson seemed to be enjoying the verbal antagonism between the two sets of brothers and kept out of the exchange.

"I admire men who rise to a challenge without using weapons, and instead prefer to use their wits rather than have such an unfair advantage," Sarah tried to ease the friction.

David snorted whilst Matt thanked her for her contribution.

Susan had watched the heated exchange and realised that there was a tension in the air that could potentially ruin the expedition.

"Weapons will only be used for self-defence, and as a last resort; anyone who thinks differently can leave first thing in the morning. There is no way that I will risk harming the creature we are hunting. Is that understood?"

"We couldn't agree more," Matt said making his support for Susan's ruling clear.

David and Wayne's reply was muttered quietly and no one could make out what they said with any certainty.

"We have spare horses that you and James can use tomorrow as we move towards the area of the closest confirmed sighting. After that I rather assumed that you would prefer to be on foot as trackers," Susan declared.

"Absolutely! You seemed to have planned everything very carefully Susan," James replied.

"My backers are not the wealthiest amongst the scientific community but they are prepared to give a woman a chance which is more than I can say for some of their more illustrious colleagues. We only have the one opportunity at this. I have to bring evidence of existence at the very least, and at best, the capture of the beast would be the icing on the proverbial cake."

"What sort of evidence will be acceptable for your scientific colleagues?" James asked.

"Oh, hair or fur samples, casts of footprints, photographs of lairs or the creature itself. Of course there is a hair sample and a footprint cast found and made some time ago but nothing has been found since to reinforce the validity of them. In truth we need the lair or the creature itself for credible rather than suspected evidence."

"How far away is the area of the last sighting?"

"About ten miles Matt, and after the first five it is all uphill so it will be taxing. The higher we go the colder it is going to get. I have brought some Inuit clothing with me for the worst of the conditions we might endure. Furs of the finest and warmest quality. They do make one appear rather bulky when wearing them though." Susan laughed and Sarah and Carson joined in.

When she stopped her demeanour took on a more serious and intense manner staring straight into James' eyes.

"Do you really think we could capture the beast without harming it?"

"There are many humane ways to set traps and capture all sorts of creatures. All are potentially harmful because their natural instinct is to try and escape and some injuries are to be expected. But our way is to be as careful as we can and once we see the creature we'll know the best type of trap to use to minimise risk," James answered carefully.

"Thank you, that is exactly what I wanted to hear and I am sure that Carson would agree with that too."

"I'm here to ensure that no harm comes to the creature, which is of course if we are lucky enough to find one. I have to warn you though there have been many similar expeditions that haven't even found the slightest piece of evidence."

"Do you have any other reason for being here apart from that Carson?" Matt asked.

"Of course I do. I'm a reporter by trade and I'm here to document the expedition from beginning to end."

"It's getting late and we have an early start in the morning, I suggest that we all get an early night in preparation for it. After tonight we will not have the luxury of a proper bed so let's make the most of it," Susan's suggestion sounded more like an order.

David and Wayne cleared away the leftover food and disappeared immediately; Sarah followed shortly after but Carson and Susan remained by the fire. Matt and James still had some food left on their plates to consume so they too stayed where they were. Carson poured himself a whisky from a hip flask and offered some to Matt and James who declined. He knocked it back in one gulp said good night then rose and went to the same cabin that the brothers went to.

"I was hoping we would get the chance to speak alone. Susan moved closer to the boys. Your reputation is absolutely impeccable and to be truthful I hadn't dared hope that I would find some trackers as accomplished as you. The fact that you don't use weapons tells me that you are probably even better than your reputation states. Either way I am grateful for having you aboard so to speak and I am going to be very forward and honest with you both. I am going to trust you with some concerns I have about the other members of the team.

"Firstly Sarah. She is absolutely marvellous as my personal assistant and I have never found her wanting. However, she is no explorer and I wonder if she has what it takes to see this through to the end. I want you both to watch out for her, as I will do myself. I would hate to see her get hurt during all this.

"Next of course is Carson. He too is not a real explorer but has the same drive that all reporters have, the need to get the story at any cost. He is likable enough and I believe he will do what he can to help, but if the going gets tough or we come up against a pack of wolves or a bear, I'm not exactly sure we could count on him. It's just a hunch but

I have had his company for a week now and he worries me somewhat.

"Then there are the brothers. They have been here a couple of weeks now and from what I have seen they are very fond of shooting and have hunted every day. They perform the tasks I ask them to but do so begrudgingly. They are two people who will place themselves first over anybody else and again I do not think I really trust them.

"I know I have only just met you both and this must sound like a comedy of errors as far as a team goes, but I need to trust somebody and as I have said your reputation suggests that I can trust you. I can trust you can't I?"

Again her eyes held theirs as she searched for confirmation.

"You can trust us completely Susan. This type of work is what we do, it's what we live for. But I have to ask why didn't you look harder for better skilled people for your team?"

"This country is still obsessed with keeping the *little woman* in her place. I tried really hard to get more qualified individuals but the top tier boffins do not have faith in women and there were actually a few who I approached, that just laughed in my face. You two were the exception."

"I think if things are to change for the better for women like you Susan then we have to make sure that we get results. Because that, more than anything, will enhance your reputation and force them to take you seriously." Matt told her.

"Thank you for that Matt. I knew I was right to choose you two."

She topped up their wine glasses a little and suggested a toast.

"Here's to our collaboration, a successful hunt and to the capture of one of the most mythical creatures in the modern world, Big Foot."

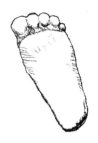

Chapter 3:
Sighting

Susan bid them both goodnight and disappeared into the cabin she shared with Sarah.

"Right, we know where we are, what we're doing here and we found that out in less than a couple of hours. Not bad eh! Can you believe this James we're on the hunt for Big Foot?" Matt gave a little whistle of excitement.

"You know we're getting really good at improvising our parts at the start of our adventures. We deserve Oscars for our performances. But yeah! Big Foot, amazing. I think it also goes by another name, I know it begins with an S but I can't quite remember it."

"It doesn't really matter Big Foot will do."

"Remember Matt we're working with a creditable scientist and as trackers we should have researched our quarry."

"Most of the stories are suspected of being made up and the so called evidence is suspected of being false. So what's there to research?"

"I agree with you but when we're with Susan we should try and be a little more scientific. She's put her faith in us so we need to give her the respect that others in this time period don't."

"Any ideas on the time period?"

"I reckon anywhere between 1910 and 1930 and that's based on the clothing they were wearing and the rifle that was pointed at us. I saw the make, it was a Winchester, but it looked like something from the Wild West."

"Susan's right about everybody else Matt. I just about agreed with everything she said about them. None of them look suitable for this kind of exploration and those brothers are going to be trouble at some point during this adventure."

"I agree, although I thought Sarah was a little braver than Susan suggested. After all she was the one who challenged us. She didn't hesitate and that rifle looked rock steady in her hands."

"I didn't notice that, maybe there's more to her than first thought."

"What did you make of Susan?"

"I liked her straight away, she's definitely determined, headstrong and a natural leader but I'm wondering if she has similar traits as you Matt. You know act before you think. No offence mate."

"None taken; would you be able to cope with two of us like that?" Matt asked with mock concern.

"I'm used to you Matt so another like you is not going to be a problem. In fact, she might be easier than you because she is so much better looking than you."

Both boys laughed.

"Speaking about looking, we should go and see how we look in this time period."

"I hope we don't have itchy beards like we did last time."

"Me too!"

The two of them rose and made their way to the cabin. Opening the door they saw that it was just one open space. In the hearth, at one end, a fire burned warmly and logs were stacked to the side of it. There were bunk beds against one wall and a table and chairs on the other. There was little room for anything else.

"There's no mirror James!" Matt said in frustration.

"Well there was a water carrier outside so all we need is a container to put some in."

"How about one of those pans that had the vegetables in, that would do."

James went outside, filled a pan, brought it in and placed it on the table. They waited for the water to still and form the mirror sheen they wanted. Then Matt thrust his head forward and angled his face above the fluid.

"Yeh, no beard. I look about thirty-fiveish, maybe forty, quite good looking really."

James peered over and could just make out Matt's reflection. He pushed him away so that he could see himself.

"We look very similar, age and looks."

Matt took a look at James for himself.

"There's no doubt that we are brothers but I think I'm better looking!"

"That's ok because it's quite obvious that I have the brains," James replied meeting the unspoken challenge that Matt had laid down.

"How on earth can you claim that, it's not something you can see in a reflection?" Matt asked.

"It's all a matter of perspective, you claim to be the best looking. That's your opinion. I actually think I am the better looking as well as being the most intelligent."

"No way James! There's no way you're claiming both."

James looked at Matt and burst out laughing. It took Matt a few seconds before he realised that James was deliberately winding him up. He picked up a pillow from the bottom bunk and swung it at his friend. Still laughing James ducked and Matt's blow missed by a fair distance. Matt started laughing too.

Both boys woke early the next morning and when they left the cabin the light was only just permeating the forest canopy. It was chilly and a heavy frost covered the ground. At these temperatures it wouldn't be long before the first snows arrived and James suspected that if they travelled uphill then they would find it sooner than later.

"I thought we were breaking camp this morning, I can't see anybody about so it's going to be a later start than I thought," Matt said sounding disappointed.

"I thought I heard voices out here a little while ago, probably the brothers, so I'm pretty sure things are already in motion."

Almost as soon as he finished saying that, David rounded one of the cabins on a wagon driven by a single horse. His brother followed with a second wagon and both stopped outside Susan's cabin. They dismounted and disappeared back towards where they had come from.

"Looks like things are more prepared than I first thought," James commented.

Wayne appeared again leading six horses, five of which were already saddled. David tied the sixth to the rear of one of the wagons. The two women and Carson Rogers appeared almost immediately. Susan spotted Matt and James and headed straight over.

"Good you are up early. I thought after your mammoth walk yesterday that you might sleep in a little, I wouldn't have blamed you if you had."

"Thank you for that consideration Susan but we're ready for action. We haven't exactly discussed what we are going to do yet but both Matt and I are sceptical about the sightings and the evidence. We both would have expected the creature to live or range at higher ground."

22

"You are right to think that, your thoughts concur with mine exactly. As a scientist I am sick of chasing down false sightings so I think we ought to start fresh. To be honest I don't even think we should start looking until we hit the snow line." Susan replied smiling.

"How far away is the snow line Susan because once we hit that it's the end of the road for the wagons," Matt said.

"The snow is about a day's travel ahead of us, we should reach it late afternoon. There are two sleds on the wagons which will be used from that point. The wagons will be left where they are. Most of the supplies will be carried by the sled but the rest will be carried by the horses. We will also leave a few supplies with the wagon in case anything happens and we lose ours or if someone gets hurt and has to return. "

"And if that happens?" Matt asked.

"If that happens David or Wayne will return with the injured person. The rest of us will go on. As I said yesterday we have only one chance to do this and I don't intend to waste it. The place of the last sighting is on route but I want to treat that with an air of scepticism. However, as a scientist it would be remiss of me not to at least have a look. Apparently the print is still there."

"Was there any fur found at or around the spot?" James asked.

"Not as far as I know."

David walked up to them. He didn't look particularly happy. Matt had noticed him moving closer to where he and James had been talking, no doubt trying to listen in to the conversation.

"We're already to go Dr," he said curtly.

"Good! There's little point hanging around, let's go," Susan said with a hint of excitement betraying her feelings.

"I'll take the lead to the place of the sighting James and from there you and Matt can take over."

23

James nodded in agreement. Susan mounted and Sarah followed her example. They didn't wait for the others and simply rode off, side by side, at a steady walk. James and Matt followed also side by side. Carson rode behind them and finally David and Wayne drove the wagons at the rear.

"The more I get to know her the more I like her James. She doesn't mess around, just gets on with it."

"I agree, but I think she gives a little more thought to it all than you do Matt."

Matt grinned. "We'll see about that as the adventure unfolds."

The group fell silent as they headed toward their first destination enjoying the peace and isolative nature of the vast forest. James wondered how far away from the nearest civilisation they were. Matt was already thinking about the next meal. It was just before eleven when Susan and Sarah stopped and dismounted at a small clearing. There was no visual sign immediately apparent to say that they were at the right place and both Matt and James wondered why they had stopped here at all.

Susan headed towards the centre of the clearing after giving Sarah an instruction. She headed back toward Matt and James.

"Susan said to follow her in," she said confidently. "Carson you are to go in too. David, Wayne, please wait here, we won't be long."

The brothers scowled, clearly not liking taking orders from Susan's assistant. Carson dismounted and followed Matt and James into the clearing.

"How on earth did you find this place in all this forest Susan? I didn't see any clues on route," James asked.

"Simple compass reading really," Susan was holding the brass covered compass up in her hand. "Come and look at this and tell me what you think," She instructed.

The boy's moved forward and crouched down beside her. There they saw a definite footprint in the ground.

"It's old, there's signs of new shoots growing through the compression. It's very human like but longer and broader," Matt said.

"Whatever made this was large and heavy. The ground is not particularly soft and yet the print is a good six inches deep. The print is at least half as long again as an average six foot tall man's," James added.

"Is it real or is it fake?" Susan asked.

"It looks real enough but..." James started before standing and moving away a couple of yards. There he jumped as high as he could and landed on his heels. He crouched down and examined the depressions he made.

"Assuming I am about twelve stone, the impression I have made is only two inches deep. Which would make whatever made that print at least three times heavier, or even more. If that print is real then we are looking for something eight to nine feet tall and weighing nearly fifty stone."

"If that's the case then there should be other prints here too because the ground is the same all around here. My stride is about a yard so this creature should have a stride length of about a yard and a half. Even if it has longer legs than our calculations then the stride shouldn't exceed two yards. There are no other prints within a three yard radius. I believe that this print has to be a fake." Matt said confidently.

"I agree." James added.

Susan nodded. "You have confirmed my own opinion too. Nevertheless, Carson photograph it, and Sarah please make a plaster cast of it just in case."

She turned away and walked back to the Johnson brothers, telling them to prepare a simple light lunch even though it was a little early.

"I want to be under way in half an hour." She said to nobody in particular.

Chapter 4:
Snow and Mountains

Susan called time on the lunch proceedings after exactly thirty minutes. She came to James and confirmed her early desire for her trackers to take the lead from this point. James reiterated that he didn't want to look for tracks until they reached the snow line and she agreed. Without a purpose beside the destination she asked the boys to increase the pace a little to ensure they had plenty of daylight left to make camp and change supplies from wagon to sleds.

Two hours later they noticed the first meaningful incline of the day and knew beyond doubt that they would exit the forest before long. The scale of the forest continued to surprise Matt and James though as it took a lot longer, than they first believed, to pass through it. Even after leaving the denseness of it there were still sufficient trees to obscure the scenery they left behind.

At four o'clock Susan called an end to the travelling the moment they passed the last tree. With two hours of light left they hadn't quite made the consistent snow covered terrain that they wanted to reach but there was enough to warrant the change to the sleds. Since the uncovered ground here was smooth any patches of it would allow the sleds to pass easily over it.

David and Wayne took on the bulk of the work. It was there job to convert to the sleds and look after the horses. The boys observed that although they were both surly by nature they didn't slack when it came to the work.

Matt and James were asked to erect the four tents, all sizeable doubles. Carson was the only one who had a tent to himself and was sent back to collect some wood for the fire whilst Susan and Sarah started making preparations for the evening meal, chopping up all sorts of things and filling a large cooking pot.

With a fire lit and the stew bubbling away, the entire group sat around it drinking hot coffee and talking quietly. The light faded and disappeared as the two women gave out generous portions of stew to the men before taking their own.

Matt was giving Sarah a lesson on tracking whilst James and Carson sat with Susan. James voiced a concern that had been building during the trek.

"We are taking a lot of horses into areas that won't have a lot of natural food for them."

"For a while we will be able to clear thin layers of snow for them to graze the grass below. A good bulk of the supplies is horse feed and we will keep them with us for as long as we can. When it gets low I shall set free all but four, two for each sled. I have always known that we will finish this exploration on foot. If and when their food runs out completely I shall release the last four. They will have more than enough time to make it back to the forest before they starve.

At this time we will also abandon the sleds and some of the less important supplies. We have seven mini sleds among our things here. They are only four feet long and can easily be pulled by each of us providing we don't over load them. Supplies to look after ourselves are the most important, food, clothing, tents etc. Specialist equipment will be ruthlessly reduced, by order of importance, and shared, by weight, among the seven of us. I will not risk harm to any of us no matter how bad I want this expedition to work."

"You've planned everything in fine detail. If all goes well, how long do you think the expedition can last?"

"Somewhere between three and four weeks: longer if we find fresh food to top up our supplies. The other thing we need to look out for is fuel to burn. If we travel at too high an altitude we might not find either, however we could travel at lower levels and make sorties to higher ground."

"I'm thinking that our creature will be doing the opposite. I think it would live at higher ground and make trips to the lower ground for hunting."

"That's my thoughts too. If that is the case then we might split our group in two. One group going up and one staying by the supplies. If the terrain gets hard higher up we won't even bother with the sleds and just have packs on our backs with the minimum of things in case we got into a whiteout or something."

"Let's hope we get something to track sooner than later then." James said admiring her meticulous planning.

The temperature was plummeting and even sitting close to the fire James could feel the chill on his back.

"I think we should all wear the furs tomorrow. We don't need anyone becoming sick or something; it will just slow us down. If the wind gets up while we are on the exposed slopes it's going to feel pretty unpleasant," he added.

"That's a good point James."

"We should rest well, eat well and keep warm and all that should help us last out for the maximum time without any problems."

"I agree and we should start straight away. Bank the fire up Wayne, it's time we all got some sleep."

Everybody was in their tent within ten minutes. The oil lamps in each made the canvas glow a faint orange and made the tiny camp seem larger than it really was."

The temperatures dropped below freezing during the night and when Matt opened the flap in the morning he was amazed how stiff it felt. James followed him outside and they both stretched. Matt placed fresh wood on the fire and placed the pot, that held the left overs from last night, above it. He filled another pot with some fresh snow and placed it by the fire to melt ready for a hot drink. David and Wayne were next to rise.

"Breakfast and coffee in about five minutes," Matt told them and for once received a nod without any sign of a sneer.

The others made an appearance just as the food was served. After breakfast each of them put on their furs and broke down their tents. Despite the fact that the furs were quite heavy, they were loose fitting and allowed complete freedom of movement. They were incredibly warm though.

For most of the day they travelled ever upward in relentless fashion. Matt and James led and kept up a reasonable pace but by mid-afternoon the snow started to become consistent and slowed them down, especially when they came to deeper pockets. The snow here was so dry that Matt couldn't make a snowball. They sank in deeply and wallowed like seals amongst rocks trying to get out. The horses seemed to sense the deeper areas and after noticing this Matt decided to walk with one of the mares at his side. When it veered to one side Matt followed and most of the deeper snow was avoided.

Carson moved to the front and walked alongside Matt.

"How much higher do you think we will need to go?"

"Not sure really, so far there hasn't been any sign that anything has been here ahead of us so I guess we keep going."

"I've noticed that the air is getting thinner."

"Are you struggling?"

"No, no nothing like that. I was just thinking that we will have to slow the pace a little if we are going higher. With thinner air it's going to be hard going."

"We haven't got to travel for much longer today Carson but I think you're right. Tomorrow we will adjust the pace."

"I noticed something else too."

"What's that?"

"Look behind you."

Matt stopped and turned. It was the first time he had looked backwards all day.

"Wow! Were you just getting me to appreciate the size of the forest or was there something else?"

"Both. If anyone gets hurt up here it's going to be very hard getting them back. Even if we were able to do that, how far away is the nearest hospital?"

"James has already spoken to Susan about this. The idea is for us to be sensible about things and prevent accidents happening. That's one heck of a view though isn't it?" Matt said trying to change the subject.

"The view in front is almost as breathtaking too, mountain after mountain getting higher and higher."

"You do realise that you might go higher here in this place than anybody else has before. Just think about the photographs you can take and the stories you can write and see in print Carson. I think you should take some here in both directions. Stop for a while and catch us up when you've finished. Our tracks will be easy to follow even if you can't see us."

Carson nodded a little excitedly, already thinking ahead about what Matt had suggested. He made his way back towards Susan who agreed and soon the group left Carson behind. Matt turned to check just as the man was unfolding his tripod. Susan rode up alongside James.

"One more hour of travelling James and then call it. How much higher before we really start searching for signs?"

"Not much. I was just thinking about something Carson said to Matt about the air thinning. Big foot, according to sightings and evidence is about nine foot tall, weighing forty plus stones and fast on the foot. A big body like that would need large lungs. If the air was too thin then it would struggle unless it had evolved to cope with thinner air."

"If it exists at this sort of altitude then I think it almost certainly will have adapted to suit the conditions which would make higher ground readily accessible. But, and this is a big but, when was the last time we saw any sign of life, animal or bird? Would this creature want to live so far away from a possible food source?"

"Could it be a creature that hibernates Susan? A creature this size should be able to store enough fat in its body"

"Absolutely, but when I researched all the possible sightings they were spread right through all of the months of the year and in such a wide area that it suggests there is definitely more than one of them.."

"Well assuming it's a meat eater then maybe it lives in more than one place during the year. Lower during the winter months and higher during the summer."

"If that's true then they creature would be thinking of moving down before the really heavy snowfall that comes about this time of year. And if that's the case then we might intercept them on route."

"I don't mean to sound pessimistic Susan but that makes everything too easy and my gut tells me this is going to be anything but."

"You're right, but I would prefer to remain realistic. It might happen, it might not. One thing is guaranteed though my career is resting on finding them."

"What would you do if the mission fails?"

"I would not be able to work again in Canada and probably not in America or England. News in the science world spreads. If the mission fails I think I would travel to Africa and work there."

"Sounds like you've everything covered Susan."

"So often in my field everything is down to meticulous detail. Anyway, there is a saying that when one door closes another one opens... I think it's about time to make camp for the night."

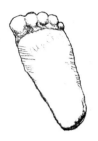

Chapter 5:
Evidence

They had already been travelling for several hours the next day when Matt's keen eyes spotted something ahead. At first he couldn't be sure what had caught his eye but as they approached he could see something red.

"Over there James, all I've seen all day is white, grey and pale blues but over there is something red."

"You're right, I can see it too."

The two boys headed off at an angle, at a faster pace, from the group that followed behind,

"Good grief look at all this. I'm guessing some kind of fight went on here, Matt suggested. Look at it, there's blood everywhere,"

"Blood, bits of remains I think; skin and tufts of hair," James responded intrigued.

"This was a fight to the death between hunter and prey. Whatever the prey was, it didn't stand much of a chance; there isn't much left of it."

"Judging by the size of the area that's been disturbed it wasn't a clean kill and the prey put up a respectable fight."

The rest of the group reached the boys position and dismounted.

"What have you found James?" Susan asked.

"Looks like a fight between predator and prey. Can you make sure nobody moves closer than where you are until we have examined every bit of this?" Matt answered making Susan address him for a change instead of James.

"Consider it done Matt," she said before barking out orders.

Carson went to get his camera whilst the Johnson Brothers scowled an answer of protest and moved as close as they could without moving past Susan's position.

James and Matt scoured the disturbed area.

"James, I've found tracks, at least one set of tracks. They came here from the right. They look like dog prints."

"Not dog Matt, wolves!" James corrected. "I'm guessing Canadian Timber Wolves. I don't know too much about wolves and I'm sure there is more than one type but it seems likely that these were Timber Wolves."

"Wolf James, wolf." Matt corrected him back as if answering an unspoken challenge. "There's only one set of prints which is a bit unusual since they are pack animals."

"Which means that this one either didn't belong to a pack or its pack no longer exists."

"Judging by the mess around here, this one doesn't exist anymore either."

"Right so we know what the prey was but we need to find out what the predator was."

"There can't be too many creatures around here that could take on a wolf and win."

"What we've been looking for potentially could."

"That's a bit of a leap James."

"I can only think of a bear as an alternative and somehow I don't think it's a bear."

34

"This is all a bit weird. There is clear evidence that a wolf walked into this spot, the tracks show that it walked here. It didn't know that something was waiting for it. The ground around is flattened which suggests that whatever else was here was heavy. But there is absolutely no evidence that anything else was here apart from that. There should be another set of prints to follow but there are none. Why not?"

"I agree Matt but I can't think of an explanation. I'm going to report to Susan and ask her to get everyone to fan out and search the immediate area; we need to widen it."

Five minutes later every member of the team started to fan out from the position of the disturbed area. They took small steps and moved slowly and deliberately, searching for the tiniest piece of evidence. Wayne gave a cry after just two steps announcing that he had a patch of fur still attached to skin. Sarah shuddered. James told him to hold on to it until they had covered the ground he wanted to search. David, searching a parallel course to his brother, announced that he too had a patch of fur. The rest of them found nothing until, after covering a distance of fifteen yards, Carson called out that he had found a single footprint moving away from the blooded area.

Everybody moved towards Carson at once, all wanting to see evidence of what attacked the wolf. Carson, who looked delighted at having been the one who found the print, beckoned everyone towards him enthusiastically.

The print was over a foot deep and was massive in its proportions. Susan magically produced a tape and measured the print at nineteen inches long. The width was a surprising nine inches and there were five human like toes although these too were in a size proportional to the rest of the foot. It was a left foot.

"Sarah, get the plaster kit and make a cast please. Take your time, make sure the print is not disturbed before the cast is made. The rest of you fan out and see if you can find the next one. We are on snow, it has to be here somewhere.

"James, Matt any further points you want to add?"

"Just one." Matt answered for the both of them. This print is fifteen yards from where the wolf was killed. That is peculiar to say the least but working on the principal that a stride pattern is repetitive then the next one should also be a further fifteen yards from this print."

"Or further. If this is the first one then it was made from a standing start the second could be even further as it settles into its stride pattern," James added.

The rest of the group, apart from Sarah, hadn't moved off and listened to the exchange with disbelief and then scorn. David expressed his thoughts.

"Nothing in nature has a stride length of fifteen yards. As trackers you should know this and yet here you are suggesting the impossible instead of following the evidence." he spat sarcastically.

"I can assure you David we're following the evidence. If you think we aren't then how do you interpret what we've seen so far?" James asked.

"Some of the tracks must have been filled in by wind or something obviously."

"That is possible, sure, but how do you explain the presence of the wolf tracks. They weren't covered up and they were much shallower than the big one. I also think that this happened quite recently, some of the blood isn't quite frozen. I think it would have frozen before an hour passed wouldn't you?"

Wayne scowled but didn't contribute anything further to the conversation. James retained eye contact with him for longer than necessary until the man looked away.

"What was all that about James?" Matt asked.

"Just a bit fed up with his and his brother's negativity and wanted to tell him so without actually saying it."

36

Matt grinned. "Should have been me psyching them out, I'm better at it than you although I have to say you did a pretty good job on him. He backed out of the eye contact in just a few seconds. Pathetic really, we've held looks in rugby matches for minutes at a time."

"Rugby seems a long way off; we keep having adventures that last for weeks, It's the only thing I miss."

"Me too."

The second print was eighteen yards away and Carson was delighted to be the one who found it again. Susan marked the spot and shouted to Sarah that there was another cast to be made. It was a right foot. They continued to search and found three more, each with eighteen yards between and each alternating between left and right before Susan called a halt to the search. They marked each one for Sarah and returned to the sleds and horses.

James questioned Susan with a quizzical look of the eyes and she moved toward him.

"I wanted to stop the search now because I don't like the idea of camping to close to where all this mayhem took place. The smell of blood could draw in more of the creatures that did this and I don't want any of us to be around if that happens. I vote we move away from here, camp, get a good night's sleep and then track this creature first thing in the morning. I also want to make camp with something solid at our backs, like rock. I want to eliminate the possibility of anything attacking us from behind during the night. The fire should be enough for guarding our front."

Wayne walked towards them.

"Here's that chunk of fur I found Dr. I'm sure it's from a timber wolf even though it's only a small sample."

"Thank you Wayne." Susan replied dismissingly.

Wayne did not take the hint and waited for her to say something to confirm his thoughts.

Susan carefully examined it before confirming the man's suspicions. He looked pleased.

"Wayne will you tell the others that we are going to move away from here and head for that sheer rock face over there. I don't want to make a camp too close to all of this. Ask Carson to wait for Sarah and photograph the casts she has made.

"Very sensible Dr," he answered and turned away.

"Did I ask for his opinion James?" Susan asked rhetorically.

"I don't think that the brothers really know how to respond to people in position. What do they normally do for a living?"

"I do not think they have a particular occupation. They take on whatever work they can get, or so it seemed to me when I interviewed them. One thing is certain though - they work hard and earn their wages. I just wish they could do it all a little more amicably."

The group made their way toward the rock face which was a lot further away than Susan had first thought. The distance foreshortened by the vast swathes of snow that were simply bigger than they looked.

Each member of the team helped with making camp and Carson and Sarah arrived shortly after the camp fire was lit. Darkness was already drawing in and the group tucked into a freshly cooked but identical stew as the one they had eaten the previous night. The likelihood was that this was to be their diet for every day unless they were fortunate enough to find something to hunt.

In their tent after retiring for the night, James expressed some concerns to Matt.

"I've been thinking and our discoveries today have changed everything,"

"How?"

"This isn't just about tracking a creature anymore because this isn't an ordinary creature. Think about it Matt. This thing attacked and killed a wolf with little more than its limbs and left almost nothing of it behind. Then the stride length. It can't be that simple. We stride at approximately a yard. Even though this creature is about nine foot tall with long legs the stride pattern is far too big. There is something here that doesn't quite add up, it's almost as if it moves like a duck trying to take off on water but never quite making it."

"Are you suggesting that it almost flies? Surely its size and estimated weight would make that impossible wouldn't it?"

"I don't know. I do know that this creature is extremely dangerous. Too dangerous to be taking a team like this one to meet it. None of them could defend themselves if it came to the crunch. My gut says that we're tracking a very intelligent creature, after all it has managed to remain relatively undiscovered for however long it has been on the Earth."

"Now you make it sound like it comes from another world."

"I didn't mean that, but it does have an unearthly quality about it."

"I get what you're saying. Changing the subject James, have you had any idea as to our purpose here?"

"No, not yet, and to be honest I can't get past the fact that we have to protect the others from this creature. Once we meet it face to face I think our troubles will begin for real."

"It's not like you to be so pessimistic."

"I'm not being pessimistic, more realistic. Everything we have discovered so far does not look good for our immediate future. Nothing is going to persuade Susan to cancel the expedition so we are going to continue. Tomorrow we are going to track this thing and the closer we get the more dangerous a situation we are going to find ourselves in. I for one am not looking forward to it."

Matt lay back and thought about what James had just said. The more he thought about it the more he fell in line with his friends thinking. He closed his eyes and fell into a restless sleep.

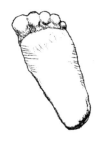

Chapter 6:
On The Trail

Heavy snowfall, that obscured vision badly enough to halt their progress, held them up several times during the following morning. At the third time of stopping, shortly after eleven, Susan called an early lunch. A fire was lit and food accompanied with hot drinks were prepared. The snow persisted throughout the lunch break and Matt suggested calling it a day and making camp if it didn't stop within another hour. Sarah made the point that the tracks they had been following may well be covered up and the trail lost completely if the snow continued but James reminded her that the tracks were almost a foot deep and as there was no wind, and therefore no drift, the tracks should still be visible.

Susan decided to give it one more try as soon as the snowfall ceased, announcing that if they had to stop one more time they would make camp and write the day off. Carson moved up alongside Matt and James after announcing he was the expert at finding the isolated footprints. The boys did not argue and were happy to have a wider landscape covered by a third set of eyes. They picked up the trail quickly and their progress was aided by the fact that the creature had kept moving in a straight line. By late afternoon a change in the scenery caused the group to stop.

"There is a high level forest ahead, I thought we were well above the tree line now and yet here we are with another forest ahead of us," Carson exclaimed delightedly.

"I agree with that Carson; I thought we'd left the trees well behind. However, I'm not so sure that this is such a positive thing," Matt answered.

"What do you mean?" Carson pressed.

"Think about it for a minute Carson, here is a forest at an altitude where nobody would have thought a forest existed. Wouldn't this make an ideal home for a creature like the one we are following? The tracks are heading in that direction."

"You could be right Matt but the tracks may yet change direction. One thing for sure is that it wouldn't be able to use such giant strides in the forest."

"True, but that could make it harder to follow because it would have to zigzag around the trees."

Susan listened to the interchange carefully.

"We are going to stop and find somewhere to camp. We cannot camp in a forest that might just be the home of these creatures. It is easy to make speculative comments and I could argue a case for continuing or stopping but the fact is that it will get dark soon where we are, and in the depths of that forest it will get darker even quicker. What do you think James?"

"I'm with you Susan, I don't want to risk venturing into the woods until we have a whole days light ahead of us. I don't want to camp too close to it either, just in case..."

"There's a sharp incline to our right, it is a little way off but easily reachable in the remaining light. We would be able to make a camp like we did last night," Sarah suggested.

"That's sensible Sarah," Susan replied smiling.

"Why don't you go and start camp preparations while James and I follow the tracks a little further. I want to see if they remain in a straight line or veer off to skirt the forest," Matt suggested.

Susan agreed and the party split up leaving Matt and James alone.

"I know you well enough to know that you have something on your mind that you didn't want to share in front of the others, tracking this further could easily wait until tomorrow; what gives?" James asked.

"You're right James and I didn't want to alarm the others. For the past hour I've had the feeling that we are being watched. It's a strong feeling and the closer we get to the trees the stronger it's been getting."

"It could be your protective instinct towards the other members of the group that is making you feel like this?"

"No, it's more than that. I'm certain we're being watched and by more than one set of eyes."

"Ok, so what do you want to do about it? We could move away from here or we could take a look further in. The others are at a safe distance away."

"I want to go in further James, I have to. But I don't agree with your last statement. I don't think any of us are safe up here with a creature that can move so fast especially if there are more of them and if they are hungry."

"If I didn't know you better Matt I'd say that you're spooked."

"I'd be lying if I said I wasn't."

James was surprised at Matt's last comment. He had never known him to admit to being scared of anything but there was something almost supernatural about the creature they were tracking. He said nothing and instead started to move forward towards the forest. They passed three more footprints before they came to the first tree.

"Well it definitely went in there." James said ruefully before asking Matt what his senses were telling him."

"We're still being watched," Matt said convincingly.

"One more track, one more to know for sure that the creature is going deeper in the woods."

They found it at the shorter distance of ten yards this time.

"It's slowing down," Matt observed.

The next was just five yards distant and then they found two prints, side by side, a left and right.

"It stopped! For some reason it stopped here Matt."

"James we need to get out of here, now!"

Matt started to move back the way they had come. Then James felt it for the first time and knew that his friend's instincts had been right. He turned to follow but before he'd taken his first step an ear piercing screech, so loud, made his hair stand on end. Both boys began to run and run fast. They burst out of the forest at top speed before slowing and coming to a stop.

"What the hec was that," James asked panting furiously.

Matt too had stopped but was looking back to the forest.

The screech came flooding from the forest again and if possible it sounded even louder than before.

"That's a warning James. It's them, telling us, not to follow them further. I'm sure of it."

"In the forest Matt, I felt it just like you, a brief moment before the first screech."

"And what about now, what are you sensing now?"

"I agree with you, it's a warning."

They stood there looking back at the forest. Everything remained as still as it had when they entered it. No sign of anything nine foot tall and capable of making that screech.

"We have a problem now Matt. Telling the others about this will spook them all, with the exception of Susan. She is going to want to continue regardless. She has too much to lose."

"It's going to be better if we don't say anything about this."

"I agree, but those screeches would have carried back towards them. They were so loud they must have heard them."

"We know that they came from the woods but back where the group is the sound would have echoed all around them. If we feign ignorance about where the screeches originated from they won't have to know the truth."

"Good idea we'll go with that."

They made their way slowly back toward the camp site as the light started to fade. When they reached it everything had been prepared for the night ahead.

"Did you hear that awful sound?" Susan asked before any form of greeting had been made.

"We did, where do you think it came from?"

"We couldn't work it out, the sound was literally everywhere! The horses didn't like it at all. We owe a debt of thanks to Wayne and David who only just managed to prevent them bolting."

The two men were still with the horses now petting, stroking and talking to them. Both Matt and James were surprised at the display of gentleness from the otherwise surly brothers.

Carson sat with Sarah with his arm around her shoulders. Her eyes were wide open and she still looked frightened.

"How far did you follow the tracks in?"

"Far enough to see them slow and come to a standing position."

"Really, you saw two footprints together."

"Yes, it was standing exactly as I am now," James answered.

"There can be no doubt that whatever it is, it moves about on two feet."

"It's my guess that it has two arms and hands too. A creature so heavy would have been standing when it killed the wolf and, unless it did it all with its mouth, it would have used hands. I still don't understand why there were no foot prints at the scene of the kill."

"I might have an explanation for that James. I wonder if the creature rolled in the snow to clean itself. There are other well-known creatures who clean in this manner."

"It solves that mystery quite nicely. Do you think the creature ate the entire wolf or carried it off with it?"

"You said the blood hadn't quite frozen when you first got to the scene so, unless this creature eats at a very fast pace, I think it took the kill with it."

Just before they turned in, Matt suggested that they posted a watch on the camp during the night. When asked why he explained that they were getting ever closer to the creature and on big game hunts in Kenya they did this all the time to protect the hunters. He added that the creature they followed would definitely be classed as big game.

Two hour watches were organised and the men took them in turn. On the third shift during Carson's watch something spooked the horses. At first they just become agitated and whinnied, then they became frantic and pulled hard at their tethers. One managed to break free and bolted. Carson did his best to calm the others but they reared up and he was forced to back away. Wayne and David emerged from their tent and immediately started to calm them down. Everybody else emerged trying to make sense of what had disturbed their night's sleep.

Matt and James took an oil lamp and followed the horse's tracks away after telling everybody else to stay at the camp.

"They are here again James."

"I can feel them too."

Then the bolted horse came at speed up the hill just in front of them. They couldn't see it but they could certainly

45

hear it. Next a loud thud that seemed to make the earth beneath them shake. A second thud further off and then the terrible sound of a horse in distress. If it was possible for a horse to scream, then scream it did, before stopping abruptly. Another thud close by them was felt in the darkness again with a second further off. Then a sound of ripping and snapping reached their ears.

"They've killed the horse James! If I'm hearing right then they are ripping and tearing it into manageable pieces to take with them! I'm not imagining this am I?"

"I don't think so Matt. The power of these creatures is unbelievable! We can't take these on with our normal tactics. We need to get back to the others, we're too exposed out here and they might decide to take us for desert."

"I'm right behind you."

Back in camp it was clear that some of the sounds the boys had heard had carried to the others. Wayne spoke to James with his opinion about what had happened and James gave him confirmation telling him to keep it from Sarah. She would see it soon enough in the morning. Only the women and Carson went back to their tents after all this. The two sets of brothers stayed seated at the fire with Wayne and David holding the Winchesters.

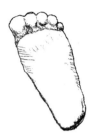

Chapter 7:
Into the High Forest and Beyond

Susan insisted on tracking the unfortunate horse before heading into the woods. It wasn't hard to find the trail and then an area of blood covered snow. The scene was identical to that at the wolf site, a completely flattened area with no tracks present apart from the horses and no remnants of the horse itself. They searched for evidence to prove that the same creatures had caused this mayhem, but none had any doubts as to what was to blame. Carson photographed the scene while the others scoured around for tracks. They found two sets, one twenty inches from heel to toe and the other sixteen. Clearly, a group of these creatures lived somewhere close and the fact that two of them managed to carry away a horse between them showed just how powerful they were.

At the edge of the high forest there was a brief pause before they moved in. Susan wanted to lead them. It was a credible move to show that she was not afraid to take the pole position. Matt argued briefly saying that Sarah would want to ride with her but Susan told her to ride with Carson. Matt and James paused before following her in.

"I can't feel their presence James," Matt said.

"I can't either."

They moved up to Susan and rode either side of her.

"I admire your unspoken gallantry gentlemen but it really isn't necessary."

"We think it is Susan and there is a selfish element to our move. As your trackers we should go ahead even if it is only a couple of yards. It is possible that this forest holds a lair and if we get too close, and there is a creature here, we might need to move fast so it would please us if you held our horses close to yours so that we can track on foot." James informed her.

Susan laughed. "What a load of balderdash! Really you two are going to are going to need to be more inventive if you think you can pull the wool over my eyes. I'm staying up front with the pair of you."

James had the grace to look sheepish and muttered to Matt that he had been deadly serious. Matt told him to try harder next time.

After passing the spot where the creature had stood feet together the previous evening, the tracks disappeared completely leaving no clue as to the direction they had taken.

"It's like they flew." Matt exclaimed disappointedly.

Susan overheard. "Did they fly or could they have taken to the trees?"

"Do you mean like the apes?" Matt asked.

"Surely they would have been too heavy for the trees, the branches wouldn't be able to support their weight." James expressed his thoughts aloud.

"High up I would agree with you but lower down the branches would be stout enough."

"I don't know, travelling from tree to tree would be slower than using their great strides," Matt countered.

"Agreed, but travelling through the trees means that there are no tracks to follow. There can be no doubt that these are intelligent creatures, they live and cooperate in either social or family groups and they have evaded capture for a very long time, so why not?"

"You rationalise very well Susan but taking the scientific viewpoint all the time might blind you from alternative thinking." James said in the most respectful tone as he could manage.

"How so James?"

"What if these creatures are even more intelligent than we are; what if, right now, they are leading us on a merry old dance, wearing us out, exhausting our supplies?"

"Humans are at the top of the ladder James; even you know that."

"But what if we aren't?"

"Well I guess time will tell, but I for one am going to need unequivocal proof of that before I could accept that."

"Let's hope I'm wrong then."

A shout from behind brought the explorers to a halt. Wayne had discovered something and something exciting judging by the way he hopped from one leg to another. The group gathered.

"What have you found Wayne?" Carson asked,

"Big Foot's trash dump by the look of it," he replied excitedly.

Bones littered the area sticking up through the snow, bones of all sizes and from different creatures. Susan picked up a femur and started to examine it. There were teeth marks all over it, marks made by a set of incisor teeth.

"Look at this, if I am not mistaken Big Foot is definitely a carnivore. I can see no evidence of any other teeth apart from incisors. It also means that this creature will have an awful smile. All the bone marrow has been extracted too. I would speculate that whatever did this used a tool of some kind, probably a stick."

Carson moved in and photographed the site then they commenced their journey through the forest. The rest of the day passed without anything else of interest. James and Matt were disappointed when Susan called time and they realised that they were going to spend the night in the woods. After the lack of sleep the previous night all the men turned in early and the two women followed shortly after.

Two more days of travelling through the forest ensued and only the compass Susan used kept them on a northward route. Without that the group would have ended up travelling in circles. At noon on the third day they finally reached the end of the forest, breaking free from the trees onto a gently rising slope. Carson again commented on the thinning of the air which suggested that their altitude had increased even more. Despite this the group moved on up the slope. No one moaned, or complained; they just kept going.

At camp that night Matt suddenly sat upright and nudged James.

"I can sense them, they're here."

It was another two minutes before James said that he could feel them too. None of the others showed any sign of sharing their intuitions though. Matt announced that he was going to check on the horses and James followed.

"I can't make up my mind if they are here for another horse or just to keep an eye on us," Matt said worriedly.

"They are here and closer than when we moved away from the others, I have a stronger sense of them now."

"Me too. I'm wondering why they haven't attacked us yet. They could at any time I know, and we'd hardly be able to put up any sort of resistance, they're just too powerful."

"I think they know we're comparatively weak compared to them and I suspect that they have learned this in the past when they have encountered other humans. I can't remember a case where a man has actually been attacked by one of these things and I wonder if we're genetically related in some way. Either that or they are simply observing us. They move at night as if they can see their surroundings so

50

they can probably see us clearly. I think they're probably nocturnal."

"You've been spending too much time with Susan because you're speaking exactly as she does James but I do agree with everything you've said."

"They've gone again Matt, I can't sense them anymore."

"Me neither. Let's go and get some sleep."

Shortly before dawn Matt and James were shaken awake by a very panicky Carson.

"What is it Carson?" James asked still drowsy.

"We've been attacked, or at least one of the sleds has, it's been trashed. I was woken by some dull thudding sounds and went out to investigate. The contents of one of the sleds are strewn about everywhere."

James lit another oil lamp and followed Carson outside. The sleds had been parked about six yards from Carson's tent and his was the closest to them. They held their lamps high to illuminate a larger area and could see their supplies strewn in the manner that Carson had told them. Matt examined the first object he came to, a sack of flour. The sack itself was unmarked and still contained all of its contents. The same could be said for everything they found.

"This has to be an attack by the creatures doesn't it," Carson said, fear evident in his voice.

"Possibly, but nothing has been damaged and if the creatures had been throwing our stuff around then I would have expected to find it further away from here." James said.

"All the footprints round the area are human and made by members of our group. There are no prints from Big Foot as far as I can see," Matt added.

"So this was done by one of us, is that what you are suggesting then?" Carson asked.

"I'm not suggesting anything yet; how long ago did this happen?"

51

"The last sounds I heard were about three minutes before I came and got you, I had a look around first."

"Well it's too difficult to see the whole picture right now Carson. Go back to bed, James and I will stand guard until dawn then we will be able to examine the site properly."

"Right, will do, I'll see you in the morning."

"Thanks Carson you did right in waking us?" James added.

As soon as Carson disappeared into his tent James walked back to the scene with Matt following.

"This wasn't caused by Big Foot Matt, I didn't feel their presence and you didn't either did you?"

"No I didn't. This mess has been made by a human or humans."

"I followed some of the tracks back to the camp site discretely and there is a set that leads from David and Wayne's tent. Could they have done this Matt?"

"They are an odd pair James but what could they possibly gain from this."

"Scare tactics perhaps."

"At best that would only end in the expedition being cancelled prematurely. All the time they are out here they are being paid, they wouldn't want that to stop would they?"

"I don't know Matt and I'm too tired to think about this anymore tonight. Let's get some sleep and look at this in the morning with fresher sets of eyes. There's nothing here to guard."

"You'll get no argument from me James but I want to be sure that we get to look at the entire area before anybody else has a chance to ruin anything by inadvertently treading all over the place."

"Can we rule anybody out from suspicion?"

"Not at this stage. We need to be open minded and not let our feelings interfere with whatever evidence is there. It's the only unbiased way to proceed."

"Let's go back to bed."

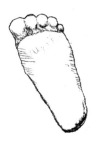

Chapter 8:
Attack

After carefully examining the area at first light there was no evidence to be found to prove or disprove who or what had trashed the sled. Susan asked to speak to Matt and James alone.

"What do you make of all of this?" She asked.

"If we are completely honest we have suspicions but there is nothing to support them."

"What are your suspicions? Come on gentlemen don't hold out on me, I've been totally up front with you."

"We don't suspect one person in particular because any of us could have done this. It's definitely not Big Foot."

"Why not."

"Firstly, there are no tracks to support its presence. Secondly, although our equipment seems to have been strewn haphazardly everywhere there is nothing damaged. Thirdly, neither Matt nor I sensed its presence during the night."

"You can sense Big Foot's presence?"

"Yes, in much the same way that we can sense a big cat's presence when we are on the trail. Our ability to do this has kept us alive for years because we refuse to use weapons on defenceless creatures." James explained in what he hoped would be an acceptable fashion.

"I would hardly call Big Foot defenceless."

"It probably wouldn't bother us if we didn't bother it."

"So how many times have you sensed it since we started this expedition?"

"Three times. The first was when the horse escaped and ran off, we felt it when we were tracking.

"And the second time?"

"The second time was when we entered the high forest for the first time. They were there, watching us. We felt them as clear as if they were actually touching us. The third and last time was when we camped after leaving the high forest. Before the sled was trashed."

"So they might have done it then?"

"No, they left well before all that happened."

"Despite the lack of evidence it all comes down to a simple choice between one of us or one of the creatures."

"That's about it."

"Humour me James, what's your best guess human or creature?"

"Human."

"How confident are you?"

"Ninety-percent."

"Matt?"

"The same."

"What could any of us gain from this?"

"At this point we have no idea but I want to keep our suspicions to ourselves and I will be watching all of them very carefully."

"I appreciate your candour."

The supplies were collected and reloaded onto the sled and the group once again started to travel, ever upward, one slope after another. Susan rode just behind the walking Matt and James, their horses secured to hers. She had taken it upon herself to keep this upfront position going for a while now, if Matt and James had this gift of sensing Big Foot then she wanted to know about it immediately. Nobody from her expedition was going to get caught.

"The bone dump in the high forest could mean that your suspicions were right about them moving down as the winter months draw in. Food would be scarcer and they wouldn't use so much energy in returning. They must burn energy at a phenomenal rate when you consider the size of them. I'm guessing that they would hunt very regularly." Matt suggested, offering Susan a chance to explain her scientific thoughts.

"I think you are absolutely correct. The fact that they need to hunt so often must mean that they cover an enormous territory in order to get enough."

"Do you think they would hunt humans?"

"Difficult to know for sure. Would they eat us? Fresh meat is fresh meat, but I have a feeling that for some reason we are not on their menu. They took the horse and could easily have taken all of us but they didn't." Susan answered.

"I guess the next question is why not?

"At this moment in time I have absolutely no idea; not even an inkling."

Suddenly James stiffened and stopped moving. He looked toward Matt who had responded similarly then turned to face Susan.

"They're here."

Susan held up her hand to stop the rest of the group still a little way behind them; they responded immediately.

"Do you know where they are James?"

"Up ahead I think."

"I can't see anything."

"I can't either."

"Stay here Susan, Matt and I will go forward and check out that mound. I can't see any other possible cover they might use to hide behind."

Susan dismounted. "I'm coming with you and it's no good arguing."

She called to the others and told them to wait where they were and then took a couple of steps forward so that she was in front of her trackers. Matt and James moved to a position either side of her.

"Do exactly what we say Susan and don't hesitate." Matt told her.

The mound was a collection of snow covered boulders that stood randomly at the centre of the slope they were travelling up. They had probably rolled down the slope from higher up and settled where they were now, possibly unmoved for centuries.

They approached it cautiously. The closer they got the stronger Matt and James sensed a presence.

"It, or they, are very close but I can't see a thing. Everything is super smooth and white and yet I know it is there?" Matt said in a low voice.

"Just one or more than one?" Susan asked in a whisper.

"Can't tell, but every hair on my body is standing on end."

They kept moving forward ten yards, five yards three yards, two yards, one yard until they reached the front edge of the mound.

"There's nothing here. Susan's whisper sounded disappointed.

"They're here somewhere, I know it." James replied.

Matt was carefully scanning the area when a gentle breeze sailed down the slope from higher up. His keen eyes saw something move. He focussed hard on the spot, staring unblinkingly.

"There James, it's there, laying over that hump. It's exactly the same colour as the snow, if it hadn't been for the breeze I would never have spotted the fact that I wasn't looking at snow but fur instead."

"I see it Matt."

"I see it too." Susan said, her voice betraying her excitement and a little too loud.

"I think you should go back Susan."

"There's no chance of that James I want to make contact with it."

"It might not want to make contact with you. Look at the size of it. The legs are huge, the body is huge, and the feet are huge. I can't make out the head because it's on the other side of the mound but I'll bet It won't have a friendly look on its face."

"I don't think this is a fully grown one James, the feet are big but I estimate only about thirteen inches long which would make this creature an adolescent."

"It's big enough to do all sorts of harm to us." Matt said ruefully.

"I can't believe we are only a few feet away and can hardly see it. Perfect camouflage and I would hypothesise that it uses this type of stealth to hunt. That wolf walked right up to it without seeing it."

"That would mean the creature doesn't have a scent." James added.

"Well I can't smell it like one can a cow or horse or something." Susan finished.

Susan took two more steps forward and reached out with her hand. She ran her fingers through the fur before pressing them deeper to feel the solid body of the creature. Matt and James watched with morbid fascination, neither spoke. Suddenly, it started to move. The back of the head lifted into view, then the shoulders started to rise and the creature started to separate itself from the mound revealing more and more of its bulk. Up and up the head rose until it stopped at about seven feet high. The width across the shoulders was more than four feet and the size of the thighs were like mature tree trunks. The thing was enormous, no doubt made larger by the depth of the fur that covered it.

The three of them kept still apart from their heads which followed the head of the creature in an upward direction. All of them held their breath as the creature slowly started to turn round. The eyes were blue, a piercing, ultramarine blue, and drew their attention at first before they saw that most of the contours of its face was fur covered too. Although the eyes were intimidating, the rest of the face did not match the ferocity. The creature stared at them before slowly opening its mouth. The gentle face disappeared as a mouth full of razor sharp incisors transformed it into a scene from a horror film. The creature expanded its chest and then let go a screech that would petrify the snakes on Medusa's head. The decibel level was higher than the base speakers at Matt and James' last school disco. When it stopped it echoed around the mountain for a full thirty seconds.

Susan, Matt and James stood their ground though all three of them trembled at the sight and sound of the creature in front of them. The creature opened its mouth again and for a moment they thought it was going to give another giant screech but instead it made a moaning sound like a child would make if it was hurt. Susan reached forward with her hand again and stroked the fur on its chest and the creature just stared. She continued until a large thud reached their ears. They turned slightly and looked along the slope. Something hurtled toward them at great speed. They couldn't make out if it was running or flying but the length of the strides and the height achieved between them was amazing.

"It's a second creature James." Matts said rather unnecessarily.

"Look at the size of it. Susan is right, this one's just a child by comparison." James answered.

The second arrived almost gliding in before hitting the ground and making it shake. It took a look at the three humans, stood to its full nine feet and let out a screech twice as loud as the other had. The noise was deafening and the three of them placed their hands over their ears. When it ceased Susan reached out her hand in the same manner as she had with the younger Big Foot but the creature extended its arm and knocked it sideways. Without pausing it gathered her up, as easily as a mother would a new born baby and held her effortlessly in front of Matt and James.

The creature stared at Matt and James who were on the verge of charging it and opened its mouth again.

"leeeeeeeeeaaaaaaaavvvvvvvvvvveeeeeeeee." It said and suddenly took off like a Harrier Jump Jet. The single leap covered more ground than any of the tracks they had followed and then it disappeared across the slope in that gliding run that ate up the ground and placed distance between them. The younger creature suddenly took off too, smaller leaps than the other but quickly placing distance between them

"Susan's gone, taken without us even having a chance to defend her." Matt said dejectedly.

"She didn't even cry out, she is so brave." James replied.

"They didn't hurt her, she may still be alright."

"But why, what good would she be to them."

"Depends on what they want."

The other members of the group came running up.

"We saw them, saw everything they did. We have to go after her." Sarah said and tears flowed down her cheeks.

"I think this is a job for James and I to take care of, we can't risk losing anybody else." Matt informed her.

"You should all make your way back to where we first met, there is nothing you can do now."

"I for one refuse to leave our benefactor out here with those creatures." Carson said thrusting his chin forward.

"What about you two." James asked the brothers.

"We were paid to do a job and we haven't finished it yet, so we are not going back either."

"Ok then. We don't have time to argue. We will follow the tracks for as long as we can. It's time to go."

Chapter 9:
Wolves

Matt and James led the despondent and shocked group on horseback, not wanting to waste a second. Both the boys were angry, partly at the creatures, and partly at themselves for not being able to have stopped her being taken. Carson rode alongside Sarah trying to comfort her with words but not quite managing to achieve it, and the Johnson brothers followed sullenly at the rear.

Matt broke the unbearable silence that had held for the past hour.

"Did you notice how incredibly fast they moved James, it's not going to be easy catching them up."

"Yes, I know." James answered shortly.

"There was something strange about their shape between their steps when they were in the air, it was different."

"I noticed that too. It reminded me of creatures I had seen on a David Attenborough film, flying squirrels. They don't really fly but their skin stretches out from their limbs to form larger surface areas and this helps them glide. There is no doubt that Big Foot's thigh muscles are enormous and are capable of achieving huge jumps and stride lengths beyond anything else I've ever seen, but when you add that with the gliding then I think that they could travel for long distances without burning too much energy."

"They wouldn't need to feed as often as we first thought then?"

"It looks that way."

"What exactly are we going to do then James because this adventure has the potential to last a lot longer than any we have been on before?"

"We have to get her back, I think that is our purpose for being here."

"That's not going to be easy."

"No it isn't but there is one thing to our advantage though."

"Like what?"

"They speak, that big one told us to leave. If they can speak then we can communicate."

"Only if they allow it."

"Then we need to find a way to make them allow it."

"We don't exactly have anything to offer them in exchange for Susan."

"Maybe we do, they want to be left alone, their existence to remain secretive."

"They could get that by simply killing us."

"That's true so maybe we have to get something that they want then."

"Like what."

"How about one of them?"

"Capture one of them! We'll never be able to keep it a prisoner, they are just too strong."

"We just need to size down a little, catch a younger, smaller Big Foot."

Matt nodded. "We've got to find where they live, find the family units before we can make any attempts at taking one."

"The risk of one of us getting hurt is going to be high so everything we do will have to be planned impeccably."

"We could just try and rescue her without all this."

"We don't move fast enough to get away safely."

"We'll have to discuss this with the others then because we are going to need their help."

"We will at camp tonight."

They ate lunch on the move so as not to slow down the pace of their pursuit. By mid-afternoon they spotted another, though smaller, high forest. As they approached it the tracks they followed suddenly altered direction and ran parallel with edge of it. To the right of their position lay an area of scree, hidden by several feet of snow, and the base of yet another mountain that offered a perfectly sheltered area to make camp. With their backs covered Matt instructed the brothers to erect the tents closer together and secure the animals against the wall of scree. James suggested two fires in front of the tents and animals. He had a feeling that fire alone wouldn't be a deterrent for a visit by Big Foot but it would make the others feel a little more secure.

James spelled out his plans to the others as they sat and ate. They listened carefully, nodding occasionally at the things he said. Surprisingly, none of them questioned the plan or placed doubts upon it. Equally surprising, was the acceptance of James as the new leader, although he never actually claimed the position.

During the night Matt was wakened by a howling of a wolf. He left the tent and stood by the fire waiting for the sound to come again. It did and the solitary howl was answered by several more. Matt ducked into the tent and shook James awake. The two of them stood outside listening as the howls became more and more regular.

"Why is it that I find the wolf howl creepier than the screech of Big Foot?" He asked James.

"There's a chance that we might be able to communicate to Big Foot but zero chance of that happening with a pack of wolves."

"They know we are here, know there are horses."

"I'm sure of it. We need to wake the others up."

David and Wayne came out of their tent armed with rifles. David offered Carson and Sarah one each as they emerged but neither offered Matt or James one. They might not have wanted to use one on the wolves but they would have been prepared to fire around them to scare them off. Matt took two long logs from the pile near their tent and placed the ends into the fire to catch light. James understood that they were for him and Matt to use as a deterrent if the wolves came too close. The howling continued and seemed to get closer and closer, louder and louder.

"They're coming Matt, they're hungry and they'll take whatever they can get, horse or human."

"Close in everybody, form an arc around the horses, we can't afford to lose them not if we want to keep looking for Susan," Matt ordered.

The howling continued as the wolves moved in until it stopped suddenly. The attack seemed imminent. The pack were coming at them from the direction of the forest. A large male led the way and at least a dozen other fully grown adults followed just behind. The leader growled gently in a low voice and the pack spread out in an arrow head formation. They moved ever closer keeping low to the ground eying the two fires that burned fiercely with the fresh wood that Matt and James had placed on them.

Ten yards away and Matt could make out the creatures eyes as they reflected the light of the fire.

"There's at least a dozen of them out there James, I can see their eyes."

"I see them too."

"Ready everybody. Don't fire until I give the word. Firing now will only deter them for a short while. They will come back." Matt instructed.

"Make sure you aim just below the head and make sure you don't miss. If we take out four in their first attack they might think twice about making a second. Aim for the middle four." Wayne called out confidently.

The horses started to whinny and move about in agitation. They knew without doubt what was out there.

The alpha male wolf growled louder, sufficient enough to be heard by their intended prey. James felt certain that the growl was the signal for the wolves to attack but suddenly a screech of terrible magnitude swept across the slope. Everybody in the group jumped at the sound and the horses started to stamp their feet in agitation.

"They're here again James. As if we didn't already have enough problems now we have them to face too."

"Deal with the wolves first," James spoke out.

The wolves knew what had made the screech but were hungry and desperate and didn't back away by the presence of a Big Foot. The alpha charged with the others following behind. Four rifles recoiled against the shoulders of the firers. In the gloom beyond the camp fires four wolves yelped at the impact of bullets to their bodies. Matt and James grabbed their flaming logs and stood facing the left and right hand side as more wolves burst into the camp.

What followed next was absolute chaos. Firstly, both the boys held their ground as two wolves leapt through the air towards them. They yelped as they clashed with the flames and received burns to their faces and Matt and James were driven to the floor under the weight of the attacking creatures. The rifles fired again with some success, verified by more yelps. Then the ground started to shake under the force of several impacts. Three huge creatures landed close by. Two swatted away the attacking wolves with effortless ease while the third knocked away the rifles from human

64

hands. The three Big Foots stood before the humans in a towering presence that made them all, except Matt and James, cower before them.

The two of them managed to find their feet and stood before the central and largest Big Foot. They stared straight into the creatures eyes and held it despite having to crane their necks in doing so. At first the creature did nothing, holding the eye contact in unflinching fashion before, as if losing patience, let out another of those ear splitting screeches. Despite the pain it caused Matt and James' ears they maintained their stares. When the noise subsided the creature lowered its head towards theirs.

"Leeeeeeeeeeeeeeaaaaaaaaaaaaaavvvvvvvvvvvvvveeeee eeeeeee," It said, as it had once before.

"Not until you return Dr Blanchett," James said defiantly.

"Return her and we will go," Matt added.

"Leeeeeeeeeeeeeeaaaaaaaaaaaaaavvvvvvvvvvvvvveeeee eeeeeeee," The creature repeated.

Then to everyone's surprise and relief the three creatures crouched and then leapt into the air. The ground seemed to shake as they landed yards away and repeated the process. Matt looked at James and James at Matt.

"They've gone," Matt said relieved at still being alive.

"The wolves have too," James replied.

"Do you realise the danger you placed us all in when you faced those creatures down?" David voiced angrily.

"Did you when you tried to point those rifles at them. I doubt that they would have done much damage if you had managed to fire them except maybe to make them angry." James countered.

"Let's just calm down a moment and let the heat of battle subside a bit before we start hitting out at each other." Carson said calmly although his body was still physically shaking.

65

"That's a good idea," Sarah said remarkably calm considering what she had just faced. I'm going to make us all some coffee with a little something extra added."

"Good idea Sarah, James and I will go and check that those wolves you all shot are not laying out their injured."

Matt picked up his and James' logs and placed them back into the fire for a few moments. When both were burning brightly they walked out beyond the camp fires and began to search for the shot wolves. After ten minutes they returned to camp.

"How many did we get?" Carson asked.

"There are no dead wolves out there. Either your bullets only injured them and they were able to go back to where they came from or the Big Foot's took the dead wolves with them. Either way it doesn't really matter because they are gone." James said.

"I know we hit more than one of them, their yelps told us that. It's hard to think that we didn't kill at least one of them," David said in a voice that was a lot calmer than the one he used before.

"Like I said, it doesn't really matter, they are gone and that's all that counts."

"I'd like to know exactly how much these Big Foots can talk because all they seem to say is leave," Carson commented.

"I think there is a lot more to Big Foot than we know and it is not going to be easy learning their secrets," Matt answered ruefully.

"There is another question that intrigues me and that is: Why did the Big Foots come back to help us?" James asked.

"What do you mean by that?" Wayne queried.

"They fended of the wolves and then just stood there looking at us?"

"They did, didn't they?" Matt agreed.

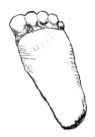

Chapter 10:
Back on the Trail

Matt and James had prepared coffee and food for the group before first light in the morning, such was their need to get moving.

"How long do you think this group will stay with us before they quit and return home?" Matt asked.

"I'd say a little longer than they would have yesterday now that they know that Big Foot doesn't want to harm us. It also increases the probability that Susan is still alive, and probably unhurt too."

"And now, in the cold light of the day, how realistic do you think we are being in trying to capture a young one."

"It doesn't matter Matt, if this was a rugby game and we were losing thirty points to nil would we quit or would we keep trying to the end? You already know the answer to your question. In a match we would move forward taking a yard at a time getting closer and closer to the try line. It's no different here. We follow the trail one step at a time. We find their home and we take a youngster to swap for Susan."

"I wonder how close we could get before they knew we had arrived."

"I doubt we could get that close. They knew about the wolves last night which means they either have ESP or they were watching our every move."

"They certainly have very good night vision."

"They do, and that got me wondering about their vision in daylight. That youngster we found, I didn't notice this at the time but he was very slow to react to us. He stared and screeched but didn't move until the adult came."

"You're right James, perhaps he didn't see us clearly but it doesn't explain how the bigger one found us."

"What if they use a different sense to see by, hearing, smell or echo location?"

"I like the idea of the echo location, they have one hell of a screech."

"Well we can't know for sure and we've only a hunch to go on but it might help us later when we get closer to them, if it turns out to be true."

David and Wayne gave Matt a nod of appreciation for the breakfast and coffee. It was the second time they had received a positive sign from them, and it was even more important now to win over their loyalty because they would probably need them to follow under some difficult circumstances in the days ahead.

The group moved out just as the sun broke between two peaks ahead of them. Bouncing off the snow, the brightness of its rays caused them all to squint, but its appearance was a welcome sight when, so often at this altitude, cloud enveloped the scene for days on end. With the mountains sloping gently now, the snow lay deeper, and Matt and James took to riding to gain additional speed. Tracking was easier too, as the footprints they followed ran straight and true. The one thing that had remained a constant difficulty was the ability to gauge the distance travelled and none of them really knew how far they had come since they hit the snowline.

For two more days they followed the trail before snow started to fall heavily and the wind picked up. Matt and James both knew about white outs but had never fully appreciated what it meant to experience one. They called an end to the travelling and set about making a camp as quickly as they could. The temperature dropped significantly and their hands were numb by the time they succeeded. With the horses tethered to a makeshift pole, rammed as deeply as possible into the snow, they all entered the relative shelter of their tents and felt the instant relief from the noise of the wind. There was no chance of lighting a fire although David and Wayne tried unsuccessfully several times. Unfortunately, they had camped where they'd stopped, exposed on an open slope where there was no respite from the buffeting wind.

For forty-eight hours they were held prisoners in their tents by the extreme weather. Taking the opportunity to rest up, they suffered without a fire and didn't have a decent meal in all that time. There was little to do and boredom was inevitable. When the weather finally broke the first thing they did was start a fire and cook up a good meal. Snow had banked up around their tents, half covering the sloping sides and as James looked around he knew beyond doubt that the trail of footprints had been buried and further progress up the mountains would be made on instinct only. As they ate he addressed the group.

"The trail has been covered, the going will be harder with all this extra snow and the only way forward is to keep to the same direction that we've been following and trust that Big Foot went home by the shortest route and didn't veer off. It's hit and miss, we might find them or we could simply bypass them and never know it. Matt and I are going to continue searching for Susan regardless but we want to give you the chance of returning before we go on. It's entirely up to you and under the present circumstances we wouldn't blame you if you did. The truth is that this is not going to get any easier."

James paused and looked firstly at David and Wayne.

"We signed on with Dr Blanchett for a period of six weeks. That time is not yet up so we are still employed. The likelihood of getting paid is non-existent if we don't find her so we're going on with you." Wayne answered for the brothers.

"Susan is not just my employer, she's my friend and I have been with her for a long time now. I can't turn my back on her no matter how difficult things get," Sarah said in a stoic manner.

"I'm staying too. I'm a journalist and this story is yet to unfold, I have to go on." Carson added.

Matt noticed that there was no reference to Susan in his reasoning.

With that all dealt with, and with a positive outcome as the result, the group started moving back up the slopes again. James followed the direction that the Big Foots had taken with a resolute and quiet stubbornness and Matt knew that if they had veered from the original direction then it wasn't by much. He kept quiet as he rode alongside his lifelong friend knowing that his company was felt even though it wasn't acknowledged.

Three days later Matt found a solitary footprint in the snow. It was semi-buried and was clearly smaller than the one they had been tracking at the start but it was heading in the direction that they had been travelling in and that told them that James' tracking had been unerringly accurate.

At camp that night David told James that the food for the horses was getting low and that he should consider letting some of them go.

"I have been testing the depths of the snow at different places in the hope that we might find a little pasture underneath for them to feed on but I have found nothing so far." David said.

"We had enough food for two to three weeks for all the horses but it was never intended that they would all stay to the end." Wayne added.

James relayed the news to Matt.

"I think we need to reassess the situation a little. There is little point in carrying the science equipment since Susan isn't here. We should dump it and go down to one sled. Let some of the horses go. Keep four. Two for the remaining sled. They can take shifts and use the other two as pack horses. We continue on foot without the burden of carrying anything."

"Sounds like you have thought about this some time ago Matt. I agree. What does everybody else think?"

Everybody agreed to the plan and in the morning some of the horses were released and one of the sleds abandoned. David asked James if he and Wayne could lead and track for a while and was pleased when James showed faith in them by agreeing. He and Wayne moved off ahead.

Carson and Sarah moved up closer to Matt and James.

"How much further do you think we will have to go James?" Sarah asked.

"There's no way of knowing for sure Sarah but I think that Big Foot is capable of travelling what we cover in a day in less than a couple of hours. Their method of travel is so much more efficient and quicker than ours. However, I have noticed that we seem to have reached some sort of flat ground that extends for as far as I can see. The mountains do go higher in the distance but at this height it looks like we might be able to move around the peaks without the need for any more climbing."

"It's as if the ravines and valleys between are completely filled up with snow."

"It does seem like that doesn't it?" Matt commented.

"What about you Carson, have you been recording everything as it happens?" James asked.

"In fine detail James, I've always thought that recording everything, no matter how insignificant, adds to the quality of the story I'll write when we get back."

Carson went on to describe the main events of his version of the expedition so far and the others listened enjoying his storytelling ability.

Matt was just about to ask him a question when he stopped and rubbed his eyes.

"Something's up ahead. One second David was there and then he disappeared," Matt told James.

James looked up and could easily see Wayne stepping confidently forward. He had been just ahead of David and so far hadn't noticed his sudden disappearance.

"Don't tell me that Big Foot has taken another of us," Susan said with no small amount of concern in her voice.

"There's no Big Foot anywhere near us at the moment, he must have fallen over in the snow." James answered.

"Or fallen through the snow."

Matt and James started to run towards the spot where David had disappeared from. As they approached James shouted for Matt to slow down and walk forward cautiously. They spotted the fissure a few yards ahead and edged as close as they dared. James lay down on the snow and inched forward until his eyes could see down into the abyss. The crevasse was much bigger inside than the entrance showed and James couldn't see any sign of David.

Wayne inched his way alongside James after realising that his brother had disappeared and guessing correctly at what had happened.

"Can you see him, I can't see him?" He asked earnestly.

"I haven't seen any sign of him. This crevasse is deep Wayne and we were too far away to see exactly where he went in."

"David, can you hear me?" Wayne called out before repeating it twice more. His calls received no response from his brother.

Matt and Carson called them and James and Wayne inched their way back carefully for several feet before standing and turning around. They each held long lengths of rope. One had been tied loosely around Matt's waist and he was in the process of adjusting it so that it raised up under his arms.

"There's no time to waste, the man could be hurt down there," he said walking forward.

Nobody argued and each of them took hold of the other end.

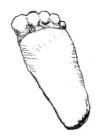

Chapter 11:
I'm Coming for You

With four of them holding the end of the rope, Matt edged carefully over the edge of the crevasse feet first. For a moment he just dangled at the top of the void looking down and felt the first shiver of fear down his spine. He knew that he was safe in their hands but the chasm was so deep; in places he couldn't even make out the bottom.

"Ok, lower me down steadily; I still can't see any sign of him yet. It's not just one hole like a well; it splits into at least four sections and I haven't a clue which one he is in," Matt ordered.

"Can you see the bottom in any of the sections?" Wayne asked him.

"Only two of them, the nearest two to where he fell in. I can't see how he possibly fell into the other ones they are just too far over. I'm going into the nearest one first; I can see the bottom about thirty feet down but it widens out and the walls are recessed a little. I can't see him but their maybe ledges or something that he might have fallen on to. Keep going until I reach the bottom, I want to make sure that he isn't buried somewhere in the loose snow."

Carefully, they lowered him until the rope went slack and Matt announced his arrival at the lowermost part.

The cavern was quite large with all sorts of ledges and shelves that could easily hold a man but there was no sign of David at all. Matt dug into the loose snow until he hit solid ice but no David. He called to the others to haul him up. He emerged from the hole and climbed over the edge.

"We need to move position for me to reach the second section. Where are his tracks again," He asked trying to get his bearings.

"They're just here roughly in the middle of the two sections you wanted to go in. I agree that the other two are too far away and even if he did fall in the deeper ones the likelihood is that we won't be able to reach him." Wayne said miserably.

Matt spoke briefly to James in a low voice.

"If he fell into one of the deeper holes I doubt if he'd have survived the fall."

The rope haulers changed position to suit Matt's next descent and once again he slid over the side feet first.

"This hole is bigger than I first thought, it has all sorts of ledges and recesses in it. If he fell onto one of them he could have rolled out of sight. I am going to have to search each ledge systematically because he might be on any of them."

"Take it easy on them Matt your weight might make them collapse or something," James warned.

"It looks likely with some of them so make sure you don't slacken your grips on the rope, if they go it will happen very suddenly."

One by one Matt started to search the ledges, it was painstakingly slow and difficult trying to get on them; several times he slipped off. Two ledges broke under his weight and sent chunks of semi frozen snow plummeting down to the floor of the cavern. The shock of each collapse made his heart race and his position changed suddenly from near horizontal to vertical. The group above were prepared for this and easily prevented him from the threat of a sudden drop and he was ready to search the next ledge immediately.

When he reached the bottom he gave those on the ropes a short break before he started searching the opposite side. Clambering onto the third ledge he found the unfortunate David at the rear laying prone and deathly still. He shouted to the others that David was there and looked unconscious and that he was going to investigate.

"Can you tell if he is breathing?" Wayne asked worriedly.

"Not with the furs he's wearing. Give me a minute Wayne," he called out.

Those above held their breath whilst they waited for Matt to confirm if David was beyond help or not. Matt edged ever closer and took off his glove. He pushed his hand out towards David's neck and searched for the spot his pulse could be felt. He moved his fingertips several times before he found it and felt it beating strongly. He couldn't stop himself from grinning with relief.

"He's alive!" He shouted. "He's in a really awkward place and I'm not going to be able to check him properly for injuries."

"How far down are you?" James asked.

"About twenty foot but there is a lot of soft snow here so his landing might not have been as bad as if he fell on the ice. Being unconscious, I can assume he hit his head hard but there's no sign of blood which is a good thing. There isn't enough room for me to check for broken bones properly so I think we just have to get him out. Do you think you could take both our weights and lower us to the bottom?"

"How far to the bottom?" James asked.

"Twenty-five feet at the most."

"Shouldn't be a problem."

"Right, I'll let you know when we are about to move off the ledge. Up to that point you'll only have my weight."

Matt wormed his way back until his feet dangled over the edge again. Grabbing hold of a handful of David's fur he pulled and it took every ounce of Matts arm strength to move him. After announcing that he was about to leave the ledge, the group above tightened their grip. Matt pulled David again and this time he was able to use his feet against the wall of the cavern to help. Once he had David's upper body clear of the ledge he held him under the armpits and locked his hands together.

"Pulling David clear now. Be ready for it." Matt called and heaved one last time.

David cleared the ledge and dangled limply in Matts grip and the two of them were lowered to the bottom. Once there Matt undid David's fur garments and checked for broken bones. They seemed fine and he examined David's head next before calling up and telling them that he had a lump the size of a golf ball on the back of his head.

"I'm going to tie the rope around David and you can pull him up first, I'll come up on the second trip," Matt told them slipping the rope around David's waist.

Then he stood back and allowed them to lift David off the ground a few feet. Matt told them to stop whilst he checked the knots again and then gave the all clear. They lifted him up at a steady pace with his arms and legs dangly below his waistline. Up and up he went rotating slightly but there was no way to stop that happening and as he reached the height of the highest shelf his legs hit the edge of it. Compacted snow and ice gave way and fell to the bottom of the cavern. Matt saw it coming but wasn't quick enough to get out of the way and a large chunk hit him on his cheek bone. The ice was sharp and dug into the soft flesh forming a gash over three inches long. He gasped at the sudden pain but looking up he was just in time to see David disappear over the edge and the relief he felt outweighed the pain. James' face appeared over the edge.

"You ok down there Matt we heard some sort of collapse?"

"I'm fine, one of the ledges collapsed and gave me a snow shower."

"The rope is coming down for you now, time to get you out of there."

The rope descended and Matt tied himself to it and after shouting up that he was ready, he was lifted out. His cheek had bled a lot and covered the side of his face making his wound seem a lot worse than it was and Sarah instantly washed it clean with some snow and placed a handful on it telling him to hold it there whilst she attended David. Wayne had already been trying to get his brother to wake up by slapping his face a little too roughly for Carson's liking.

"Take it easy Wayne we don't know how bad his head is injured."

Wayne's reply wasn't too polite and went something along the lines of mind your own business. His tone changed when his brother opened his eyes.

"He's conscious," he said and moved aside for Sarah to check the lump on the back of his head.

She asked him a few basic questions and his answers showed that he was understanding everything she asked. She bandaged the head even though there was no open wound. When she finished she went back to Matt leaving David alone with his brother.

The snow on Matt's face had all but melted and again she washed away the fresh blood with snow.

"The cut is long but not as deep as I first thought Matt, I don't think it needs stitching. It seems to have stopped bleeding now and I think it is best left open to the air. It's not likely to become infected in this climate. With any luck it won't leave a scar either. By the way I think you were very brave going in after David like that."

Matt thanked her and James came over to check his friend for himself.

"You've had worse than that on the rugby pitch, you'll live."

"Thanks for those words of comfort James."

James grinned and Matt grinned back. "Seriously pal, well done down there."

Matt ignored the comment and told James that they should make camp early and give David a little time to rest before they had to start moving again. James pointed ahead to the next large peak.

"We'll camp over there well out of the way of this crevasse."

The group moved and made camp then spent a light hearted afternoon telling stories. Each of them were acutely aware of how fortunate David was not to have been more seriously hurt, and just before they all turned in for the night, David walked over to Matt and thanked him for everything he had done to rescue him and then shook his hand. His brother nodded his appreciation too and Matt knew that he had won the two men's respect. Perhaps now there would be less friction between the two sets of brothers.

Chapter 12:
The Warning

The swelling on David's head had reduced by the next morning and he declared himself fit to travel. James asked Sarah to check him over to make sure he was as fit as he claimed and she came back with confirmation that he had suffered no ill effects from the fall. Twenty minutes after the sun came up the group were on their way again but the ever upward direction was starting to take its toll on them all now. With significantly thinner air and lower temperatures it required greater physical effort to keep going as they laboured with their breathing; their progress now was a testament to their determination and drive. James called additional rest stops between their customary food breaks but they were short, barely enough time to recover from panting. The remaining horses were labouring too and it was only a question of time before James would have no choice but to set them free.

Late that afternoon the slopes levelled off forming a plateau area between three very tall mountains. The flat terrain was huge stretching for several miles in each direction. James called Matt over when he discovered another set of footprints traversing the area in the same direction as the ones they had been following.

"I'm starting to get the feeling that we're getting close. Although it's not a strong feeling, they're close I'm sure of it. How about you?"

"I've been feeling the same for the last hour or so. At first I put it down to wishful thinking because I have to say I've just about had enough of this constant uphill slog. The feeling increased as we came over the rise. There has to be a limit as to how high Big Foot lives. I know they can travel fast but there hasn't been any possible food sources for them for at least the last two days."

"We've never really thought about the type of home Big Foot might have. There are no more forests up here so perhaps they live in the open. Their fur was dense enough for Susan to conceal her hand in when she stroked the younger one."

"What about caves James, ice caves. Up here the snow will last all year round and is probably very deep against the sides of the mountains. They are big enough and strong enough to make them. The certainly have the intelligence!"

"I'm just looking at the mountain straight ahead of us. It's probably three or even four miles distant and just as you mentioned caves I'm sure I saw something like that. The sun was shining across the face of the slope and there was just a hint of caves before it disappeared behind clouds."

"Why don't we call a rest stop and just wait for the sun to reappear?"

"Good idea, because if they are caves then I don't want to get too close them just before nightfall."

James called the break and the group behind them, who had just about caught up, sat down heavily on the snow. The horses stopped without instruction.

"We are going to be quite isolated out here when we stop. There's nothing to camp against unless we walk to one of these mountains. If the wind picks up then it could be quite an uncomfortable night."

"I'm thinking that we should go back and camp just below the plateau line. That would at least afford us with a slope at our backs."

"Let's do that James in case our theory is right."

"Well here comes the sun again."

The two of them stared hard as sunlight bathed the mountain in question. From its low angle and position sideways on to it was clear that there were darker areas of shade that resembled caves, lots of caves.

"I see them too James, you're right, I'm sure"

Wayne suddenly appeared by their side.

"I was going to ask you where we're going to camp tonight but seeing the direction of your stares I think I have my answer. Are they caves, they certainly look like caves?"

"Thanks Wayne, you've just confirmed what we thought."

"Are you thinking of camping in one of them tonight because I'm not sure we have enough daylight to reach them in."

"We thought that too but were thinking that these caves might already be occupied."

"Big Foot?"

"Makes sense if you think about it."

"It does, natural shelters, caves. You're not thinking of moving closer to them now are you?"

"No we'll camp below the plateau line and use the slope to conceal us."

"The slope might do that but they will see the glow from our fire for certain."

"They know we are here already, I'm sure of it. They might not have good sight during the daylight but their other senses are keen."

"Shall we tell the others James?"

"You can tell David but hold back with the other two, there's no need to worry them yet. We don't even know for sure that these caves are inhabited."

"Right I'll do that." Wayne said and moved away.

"We have ourselves a team member at last."

"Yes we do. I'll tell you what though Matt, I'm as sure as I can be about Big Foot being in those caves."

"I think you're right."

The group headed back off the plateau and set up camp. David prepared the fire and Matt noticed that he set it deeper into a snow hole.

"It will reduce the amount of glow it gives off. Might not give away our presence unless they are out looking for us."

"Good idea David, well done."

Sarah and Carson busied themselves preparing food and talking quietly enough not to be overheard. Matt and James had noticed their friendship developing. Carson insisted on pampering Sarah at every opportunity and clearly his efforts to gain her affection were succeeding. David and Wayne were taking on more than their fair share of work, which they always had done, but were doing it a little more cheerfully. Both of them had said more to the other members of the expedition in one day than they had for the past week. The team had cemented through trust and mutual respect for each other's skills.

It was about half past one in the morning when the peace of the night was shattered by a deep rumbling sound. All of them were wakened by the sound which was getting louder and they emerged from their tents.

"What is it?" Sarah voiced the question that nobody knew the answer to.

"Sounds like an earthquake or avalanche." Carson suggested.

"It's not an avalanche we're on the edge of a plateau." Matt said firmly.

"I'm not sure we'd hear an earthquake at this altitude. We might feel one though. Wayne added.

Then both Matt and James stiffened.

"Get the guns David. The Big Foots are here and there is more than one of them." Matt shouted.

David fetched the weapons and this time brought enough for Matt and James to have one. Reluctantly they each took one.

"Fire only at their feet or above their heads. Only fire if they try and harm one of us." James ordered.

"Form a line with me. They are up on the plateau." Matt instructed and the others did as ordered.

The rumbling stopped and suddenly a deathly silence reigned over the area. The quiet had a more terrifying effect than the rumbling and each of the group was shaking with a mixture of fear and anticipation. They craned their heads at an angle trying to hear something that would give away a Big Foots position. Then came a loud thud directly in front of them. Another to their left, then one to their right. Several more came from behind them and then more in front. Thuds rained down all around them like dulled machine gunfire. Each of the group knew they were surrounded and James ordered the line to move into a rough circle. Trembling they moved to the instruction holding their Winchesters poised for action.

A shorter series of dull thumps followed and a nine foot tall Big Foot walked into the lighted area of their camp stopping just a few feet from James. The Big Foot pushed his head forward and let loose a screech loud enough to be heard for miles. Still the group remained still and held fire. The Big Foot screeched a second time and all the other giant creatures positioned around the camp joined in. The noise was deafening and the group were forced to cover their ears and effectively removing their weapons from their targets. When the noise finally subsided the Big Foot in front of James took another step forward. Matt turned slightly so that he stood alongside his friend.

"Weeeee tollllllld youuuuu tooooo leeeeaaaavvvvvvvvveeeee." The creature said.

"And we told you that we wanted Dr Blanchett given back to us." James said defiantly.

"I hope for your sake that you haven't hurt her." Matt added staring coldly at the creatures eyes.

"Sheeeeeee hassssssss nottttttt beeeeeeeeeeeeeen harmmmmmmmmed."

"Then give her back and we will leave." James replied.

"Yooooou havvvvvvve seeeeeeeeen toooooooo mucccchhh."

"We can forget what we have seen if you give us back Dr Blanchett."

"Yooou willlllllll commmmmme wittttth ussssssss."

There was a movement behind them and either Wayne or David fired their rifle in the air. The entire group of Big Foots screeched again. When it ceased Matt asked why they had fired.

"Creature moving closer. Thought I would give it something to think about. Fired above its head."

"Yooooou willlllllll commmmmme wittttth ussssssss." The creature repeated.

"We have just demonstrated our answer." James replied angrily.

Then the big foot crouched slightly and jumped temporarily disappearing from view. He landed by the camp fire, bent and picked up the unburning end of a large log. He then moved away from the fire and held the log aloft. The flame sent enough light to show the presence of a wall of Big Foots that extended completely around the campsite.

"There has to be at least thirty of them surrounding us James." Matt commented softly.

"I'm guessing that these are just the males. There isn't one here as small as the one Susan encountered."

"I don't know what the collective name is for a group a Big Foots so I am going to call it a colony. This colony is far bigger than I expected. There are far too many to take on in any kind of fight so it looks like we have little choice but to go with them."

"They might think twice if we took a couple out with the rifles James." Carson suggested.

"I think that if we did that then they will take us out and they wouldn't need rifles." Matt answered.

"Break camp and load up the sleds, were going with them." James ordered.

"Have you lost your mind James?"

"You can stay and fight if you want Carson but I haven't forgotten what my mission is and this seems like the best thing to do under the circumstances."

"If we go with them, we might be kept or worse."

"If we go with them I think we'll find Susan because despite all their strutting and screeching they haven't harmed any of us so far and I'm betting they haven't harmed Susan."

"I don't fancy the odds on that bet James."

"I'll take it," Wayne said.

"Me too," added David.

"I don't fancy trying to fight these things Carson they're huge and too powerful for us," Sarah said timidly.

Carson looked completely bemused by the groups support for James. "We'll regret this James."

"Not if we live to see another day Carson."

The surrounding Big Foots waited patiently, without moving as the camp was packed away. Then Matt and James led the group off in the direction of the mountain of caves without any regard for the creatures around them. Then quite unexpectedly, and as if the creatures had suddenly lost patience, they moved in on the members of the expedition, plucking them up like they were feathers and launching into their flying runs. There were screams and shouts from the humans but they were ignored. Some grabbed the horses and some the sleds, nothing was left behind.

James bizarrely found himself enjoying the new travelling method. Although he could see nothing, he felt the power of the creature's leaps and then the long soaring flight before they touched the ground again and repeated the process. He felt the creature's body stretch as the skin beneath its arms and between its thighs extended, broadening its shape during the soar and then retract as it touched down again.

Again and again the process was repeated until it finally stopped as they reached their destination. The Big Foot let James down and leapt away before one by one the others were released too.

"That was a very different way to travel James." Matt said ruefully.

"It was and I would estimate that we have just covered about four miles of travel in just a few minutes if we are at the caves," James said.

"There seems to be a light up there James, the only one around here. It could be Susan!

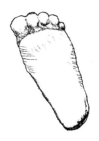

Chapter 13:
Big Foot Revelations

The others gathered around Matt and James after being dropped off in the same manor. Carson complained indignantly about being manhandled until David told him to quit moaning as they had all experienced the same treatment. Carson glowered but held back from further comment.

"Now what? They've just dumped us in the middle of nowhere and left us. They must be really confident that we are not going to escape from here," Wayne stated.

"You can't blame them for feeling that. Where would we escape to? At the speed they travel at, they could catch us whenever they wanted. They could give us a week head start and still catch us before we left the snowline."

James ended the pointless discussion by asking if they were all unharmed and was relieved when each of them reported in positively. Standing there, silhouetted against the snow, and on the far side of the plateau, there was little they could do until daylight illuminated their location and the true number of Big Foot creatures they were up against.

"What are we going to do now?" Sarah asked.

"We are going to walk towards the only light source around here. Matt and I noticed it the minute we were put down. Luckily, we were facing the right direction."

There was no point James pointing, it was too dark for the others to have seen the gesture but they all turned until they spotted the light.

"Looks like a fire to me, the light is flickering. Since I can't see the flames I can only deduce that it is in one of the caves we saw earlier," Carson stated.

"Follow us," James ordered and walked towards the light.

Nobody argued and the group moved off. The fire was further away than they first thought, the glow coming from the cave mouth looked brighter than it really was because it was the only thing visible in the dark. Just as they reached the entrance the walls either side of it moved. James and Matt halted in surprise and those behind bumped into them.

"What is it?" Carson asked.

"We're not alone," Matt said as the moving walls formed into the more familiar Big Foot shapes.

Easily nine feet tall they were amongst the biggest they had come across so far. They stood motionless on either side of the entrance. At first James wasn't sure if they were there to prevent them going in or encourage them to do so. He made his decision easily, he and his group needed the light and the warmth of the fire and he needed to know if Susan was inside. He moved forward again and the others followed. The two Big Foot made no attempt to stop them but moved in front of the entrance the second they had all passed through, effectively blocking it with their mass and preventing any opportunity for them to leave.

The cave was narrow but high at the entrance before forming a tunnel that disappeared around a bend. The effect from the flickering fire could be easily seen, dancing on polished walls, walls of solid ice. It was close, just around the turn, and James didn't hesitate to take the few paces required to reach it. The tunnel opened into a circular shape with a domed ceiling almost like the inside of an Inuit igloo except for the fact that there were no sign of ice bricks. The curved wall was polished ice just like the tunnel that led to it. It caused a slight mirror effect making the space seem bigger than it really was.

The fire burned brightly but gave off no smoke and James wondered what fuel was being used as there was no sign of any wood. Behind the fire a bed of sorts had been made on the floor with a selection of furs and a single human sized body lay buried among them. Matt moved around and pulled back a fur to reveal the long blonde hair of Dr Susan Blanchett. He placed his hand on her shoulder and shook her gently.

"Susan, wake up."

She stirred turning on to her back after a second wakeup call reached the slumber filled numbness of her mind and encouraged her to open her eyes. She stared at Matt's face looking down at her for a brief moment before her senses completely kicked in and she sat up.

"You're here, all of you," she said looking around at each of the group in turn. "How did you find me or should I be asking where did they find you?"

"We tracked you to the edge of the plateau before they came to us and brought us here. How have you been, have they hurt you, tortured you or anything?" Sarah asked.

"No, nothing like that, to be honest they have been really good hosts and have given me everything I need for a stay here. But before I tell you more I want to hear about your journey here."

Sarah and Carson filled in all the details of their plight since Susan's abduction.

"Sounds like you have all had the most adventurous of times. I'm amazed that you have been able to track me to this place though. When Big Foot moves at speed they don't leave too many signs behind them."

"Tell us what you have learned about these creatures Susan?" Carson requested.

Before she could start a smaller Big Foot entered the space carrying a huge bundle of furs. It sheltered its eyes from the fire and dropped the furs immediately turning and leaving.

"Thank you Brond." Susan called.

"They have names?" Sarah asked in surprise.

"They do but they are virtually unpronounceable so I do what I can with them by shortening the sounds they make. Brond is only the first part of a very complex group of sounds that form her name."

"Brond is a female, how can you tell?" Carson asked.

"The males have black noses and the females have brown tones to theirs. It's the only visible difference."

"What do they want from or with you Susan?" James asked.

"First and foremost they want to be left alone. They know far more about us than I first thought which results from long periods of observing us. They are naturally inquisitive but recent sightings of them by humans has brought party after party of explorers who want to catch one to prove their existence."

"How do they feel about that, especially in the light that we are just such a group?" Matt asked.

"They understand the need to find out about things of mystery and there have been times in the past where humans, having found Big Foots, have stayed to learn more. Big Foots, in the same situations have studied humans too. A mutually tolerant and open exchange of cultural understanding. The humans never returned to their own kind though."

"From choice or because they weren't allowed to go?" Carson asked.

"Choice, I'm told, and they have given me no reason to doubt their honesty."

"When they came for us they told us that we have seen too much," Wayne informed her.

"Yes, too much without having the benefit of putting everything into context."

"What do you mean?"

"Well, tell me what you have learned about Big Foot so far."

"Apart from obvious things like size and description we know that they are nocturnal, meat eaters, capable hunters and how they move – run and soar," Wayne continued.

"Nothing you have described so far has made them appear like the incredibly complex and social creatures they are. On the contrary I think. So far you have described them as freakish monsters. Something to be feared. And this is typically what everybody, that encounters them, portrays," Susan interrupted.

"Since arriving here though I have learned that they can be incredibly gentle, think of how they handled you, they have just provided you with furs for sleeping on. I didn't ask them for this and neither did you. Surely, that makes them considerate. They can communicate in English which makes them intelligent and capable of learning. They are extremely social, living in extended family groups and have a hierarchy system just like we do. Now that is starting to alter your perception of them isn't it? Unfortunately, none of this ever reaches the ears of the humans and even if it did, it would be met with fear and quite often a lack of compassion," she continued.

"I agree with what you are saying Susan, fear of something often invokes a negative response that sometimes results in violence. You however, seem to have communicated with these creatures over the last few days and reached some sort of understanding," James stated.

"I have been treated like a guest here. Every need I have had has been met with consideration and concluded positively. In exchange they seek knowledge of us as a species in the same way we do them. I can't tell you how exciting it has been to learn about their history as a species and see their excitement as they learn about us. They believe that at some time in the distant past we were related but followed different paths of evolution. They learn as fast as we do and everything is shared as stories. The aboriginals in Australia pass on their history through stories in the same way."

"At the moment Susan I for one don't feel like sharing anything with these creatures because I have been brought here against my wishes and I am nothing but a prisoner here," Carson said with more than a hint of anger.

"You'll have a chance to talk to them during daylight hours. They all retire to the caves in daylight only venturing out if forced to. The light hurts their eyes. The reason they are not here now is because they are out seeking food," Susan explained.

"You mean to say that if I wanted to I could just walk out of here."

"You could but I wouldn't recommend it, the plateau is riddled with fissures. Fall in one of them and you are unlikely to be able to get out by yourself and it is doubtful if you would ever be found."

Carson looked annoyed. "So I am a prisoner by way of location."

"Only if you want to see it that way. Look it's late, why don't we get some sleep and talk about this more when you've rested."

"That sounds sensible to me but I need to ask you another question before I turn in."

"What is it Carson?"

"I could be wrong here but I get the impression that you want to stay here for an indefinite period. Your enthusiasm for these creatures is obvious and while I can't blame you, as a scientist, for wanting to stay and study them, it's not exactly what we signed on for."

"You are correct Carson. I do want to stay and I have formed a partnership with Ditan the alpha male here for a mutual cultural sharing of information. It was my thoughts that you would all give up searching for me and return home. I did not expect such resolve from you all. I am flattered of course, but I don't want to keep you here against your wishes."

"Aren't you worried about what we might say when we go back?"

"Not at all. For the most part anything you said would be met with severe criticism and disbelief. You wouldn't be taken seriously. You have nothing of any proof apart from some plaster casts of footprints which could easily be faked."

Carson felt angry and betrayed. "One last question. Why did these creatures take you and not one of us?"

"This is not the first time I have encountered Big Foot Carson. For the very same reasons as I have just stated I could not discuss anything about my previous encounter because I wouldn't have been taken seriously. Ditan's son Donek was the Big Foot I stroked down the mountain. He recognised me from two years ago when we first met. Ditan recognised me too when he came for Donek. It was he who carried me away from you all. Now let's get some sleep.

The conversation died at that point and the group spread the furs and settled down for the remainder of the night.

James whispered a few words to Matt. "Did you believe all that?"

"I'm not sure."

"Me neither. We're talk about this in the morning."

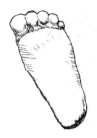

Chapter 14:
Guests or Prisoners

Both Matt and James were unable to close their eyes in what remained of their disturbed night but despite their lack of sleep they were both up before dawn and before any of the others woke.

"I want to go outside so that we can talk without the others present," James whispered.

Matt nodded before adding. "I guess we'll find out now whether we are guests or prisoners then because last thing I remember about coming in here were the two nine-footers that moved in front of the entrance after we all entered."

Quietly, they moved away from the rest of their group and rounded the bend toward the entrance. The two Big Foots were still covering the entrance. Both turned to face them as they approached.

"We wish to go outside for some fresh air. We will not be going far and shall return when we are ready," James said in a firm and confident manner.

At first the two creatures stayed still but then, without any noticeable communication between them, they parted allowing the boys through. They walked about twenty yards away before Matt spoke.

"Nice one James you sounded like you were their leader."

"A little bluff Matt and to be honest I didn't think it was going to work."

"Well it did and for the moment we are alone. I have been thinking about what Susan told us last night and to be honest I just don't get it. Why didn't she tell us about her previous encounter with the creature? In all other dealings with her I have always thought she had been up-front and truthful with us but now, now it casts doubt on everything."

"I know what you mean Matt but if I was in her shoes I don't think I would have told anybody else about that encounter either. Think about it, nobody would have taken her seriously and the most likely outcome would have been the cancellation of the expedition."

"Did she plan to stay all along or is that just a result of what has happened do you think?"

"No way of knowing that for the moment, but if she had pre-planned a stay I'm not sure when exactly she was going to tell us."

"She didn't seem to have been too bothered by the idea that we might have quit looking for her and left her out here."

"Probably because she feels she is safe with the creatures."

"She isn't going to be worried if we all go either."

"That's assuming that we are free to leave."

"If you were in Big Foot's shoes, so to speak, would you let us go?"

"It's an interesting question Matt. They are clearly intelligent creatures, far more than anybody could ever have guessed. They know they are powerful, fast and clever enough to evade human contact whenever they chose to do so. They must also know that humans have weapons that could potentially harm one of them. Assuming what Susan told us last night is true then they know that any stories we take back with us would make us the laughing stock of Canada. Nobody is going to believe any of this, not without proof and we just don't have anything to back it up, any of it. Carson wouldn't run a story on this, I'm sure for the same reason. Anything Sarah said would be treated the same way and as for the brothers grim, they would keep all this to themselves, they'd have nothing to gain from it.

"On the other hand you have to ask what they could gain from keeping us. There are only two reasons that I can think of. The first is to learn from us; they already have Susan so I really don't think they need us too."

"And the second?"

"Food!"

"Really James?"

"Why not, they are meat eaters after all."

"You don't really think that."

"You're right, I think they will let us go."

"What about Susan?"

"She's old enough to make her own choice and the rest of us should respect that. If she wants to stay then so be it."

"So when will we be leaving?"

"Well I thought our mission here was to look after Susan but now I'm not so sure what it is. I think we should stay for a while, learn a little more about these creatures and how they live and see if anything else comes to light."

"We might get some opposition from the others about this."

"I don't think so, Carson would want whatever he could get for his story and I am pretty sure he would persuade Sarah to stay with him; they seem to be getting close. The

Johnson Brothers are on the payroll so I don't think they would be in any hurry to leave either."

"That makes sense. I suppose we should get back to the others and get ready to meet some of these creatures face to face. That, more than anything else, should tell us how things are going to go. You know we have done some amazing things since we started coming through the portal but sitting down and having a conversation with Big Foot rates right up there in the list of bizarre."

They both laughed and shook their heads.

"Whatever next?" James asked rhetorically.

The boys went back to the cave and the two Big Foot guards moved aside to allow them entry. The group were already up and something good was bubbling in a pot beside the fire.

Susan offered them a cup of coffee each and they took them gratefully.

"I'm going to arrange a meeting for us all with Ditan when he returns from hunting. It will be his decision if you are all to stay a while or return home," she said smiling warmly.

"Surely, that is our decision to make?" Matt said defensively.

"Yes and no. You can make whatever decision you want but it is Ditan who will ultimately either allow or deny it. This is his domain and he is the leader. He rules as a king; it's not a democratic society. Whatever he says, goes."

"We didn't ask to come here, he forced us."

"I know Matt, but the protection of his group is of the utmost importance to him. I'm sure he brought you here so that this can be sorted out in an amicable and non-violent way."

"Perhaps he should have tried asking. If he's so intelligent why didn't he just try to meet us like anybody else?"

"They are not human like us and their way of doing things is not quite the same as ours. It might sound a little dated in the way they do things here but they live in peace, have everything they need and there is no social unrest. I think we could learn something worthwhile from that."

James noticed that Matt wasn't liking Susan's comments very much and intervened.

"I think meeting Ditan is a good idea; how soon can you arrange it Susan?"

"I will speak to him as soon as he gets back. I feel sure that he will talk to you all before he rests up for the day."

After breakfast had finished Susan disappeared to speak to Ditan. Matt and James filled the others in on what had been said earlier. At first there was more than a little hostility towards the Big Foot for bringing them here in the first place but James worked hard to dispel their fears about being prisoners despite the fact that he wasn't quite sure what their status was.

Susan returned after half an hour and told the group that Ditan would be here soon. For the next few moments nothing was said as they waited for the thud of Ditan's footsteps to warn them of his arrival. The thuds came and the biggest Big Foot of them all entered the cave and sat down opposite the group who had moved closer together. He sat there silently staring at them as if trying to weigh each of them up to discover if they were friend or foe just as the group were doing to him. After a tense few moments Susan broke the silence and introduced each member of the group to him, not only by name but also by their role in the expedition. Then she introduced him to the group as King of the Sasquatch. Ditan and the expedition members still didn't speak and the silence started to get a little uncomfortable before Carson spoke first.

"It's a pleasure to meet you King Ditan. I never really believed Big Foots existed until a few days ago and now as I sit opposite one I am so pleased to able to converse with you."

Ditan turned his head toward Carson slowly as he spoke.

"We are known as the Sasquatch!" he started. "You will tell others of your kind about us?" He asked in a deep voice that bore no resemblance to the voice he had used when telling them to leave.

The voice carried a trace of accent but unlike anything they had heard before. The words seemed almost laboured, drawn out as if spoken under extreme effort.

"I would sir. All humans should be told about another civilisation that lives alongside us but in seclusion from us."

"What would you tell them?"

"Why, how amazing and how intelligent you are as a species of course."

"What if we do not want to be known to your world?"

"There is plenty that can be gained by collaborating with us. Think about it for a moment, the combining of two cultures, the sharing of skills and resources."

"We have no need for this and we already know about you as a people." He turned his head slowly and deliberately toward Sarah. "What would you tell the humans?"

"Nothing! I am Susan's friend as well as her colleague and although she told me about her previous encounter with you, I am ashamed to say I didn't really believe her. I thought she had dreamt it or something.

"Sorry Susan, but it all sounded so bizarre until now."

"I understand Sarah, don't concern yourself with it." Susan offered gently.

Ditan turned towards the Johnson Brothers. "What would you say?"

"Nothing, nobody is likely to believe a story like this without proof and we don't have any. It's better to keep it all to ourselves." David answered for them both.

"You use weapons; would you use them on the Sasquatch?"

"If you were attempting to harm any of us I would definitely use them. They are for protection and the hunting of food." Wayne spoke up honestly and Matt in particular admired his forthright nature.

"Would you hunt the Sasquatch for food?"

"You are too like us to consider you as a food source so the answer has to be no."

Ditan turned his head again this time toward Matt and James.

"You do not use the weapons, you track with skill creatures that can harm you but you do not use the weapons. Why is this?"

"Everything has a right to live. We tracked you because we wanted to learn about you. We don't want to harm you," James answered.

"What we want to know right now is if we are free to go or are we prisoners here?" Matt asked pointedly.

"We want to learn about you as you do us; we also do not wish to harm you."

"Then why did you take us last night?" Matt demanded.

"We took you because you did not give up looking for Susan and because the plateau has many crevasses. He was lucky when he fell into one and you were brave in saving him." He said pointing at David and then Matt. "We did not want to see any more of you fall below the snow."

"Are we free to go or are we prisoners?" Matt searched for the truth around their presence here.

"You are free to go but you will stay for a few days."
"Why?"

"The weather is about to get worse. Snow for several days with high winds. Travel in those conditions will be dangerous for you."

"Who taught you to speak English?" James asked.

"There have been many humans who have stayed with us in the past. Your language is easier for us to learn than ours is for you. I will go now to rest but we will talk again. You may leave the cave as you wish and explore but do not disturb the Sasquatch who sleep."

With that Ditan stood up and left the cave.

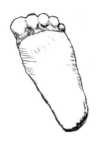

Chapter 15:
Trouble

For almost a week the group found themselves more or less confined to the cave as blizzard conditions kept the world outside obliterated by a whiteout. Frustration and boredom set in and everybody became irritable and short tempered. The Sasquatch came and went in their usual manner using other senses than their eyes to continue hunting but had kept their distance from their human guests. Having only been summoned twice during their temporary confinement, even Susan's patience was being tested. Matt and James had withdrawn slightly from the group and had been given a cave of their own to use after making a not completely honest complaint that there were too many people in such a tight space.

When it finally stopped snowing on the morning of the sixth day, the Johnson brothers came to Matt and James to let them know that they had decided to leave. James was not surprised, the brothers had been idle for too long and could see no purpose in remaining. They had helped Susan find the Big Foot, or Sasquatch as they were now called, so their work seemed done. They wanted to go home and once again find some normality in their lives.

"Have you told Susan yet David?" Matt asked.

"No I wanted to see and tell you first; I owe you my life and it's a debt I'll probably never get the chance to pay back so call it a courtesy if you like."

"You don't owe me anything David; what I did was what any decent person would have done, but thanks for the thought," Matt replied.

"Have you told Ditan yet?" James asked. "I, for one, am not totally convinced that I can trust him yet."

"We are going to see him next."

"I'd like to come with you if that's ok, I want to see his response. I want to see his manner in a situation that has nothing to do with Susan." James added.

"You trusted Susan and now you are not so sure are you? We share the same doubts. By all means come with us," Wayne answered.

The four of them went to Ditan's cave. There was no difference between his and any of the other Sasquatch caves. A single space opening to the outside world with a smaller than expected entrance. There was no light source or fire inside the dwelling. He was not alone though. A female and two young Sasquatch were also present and James took them to be his immediate family. Ditan rose from a crouched position as they entered.

"There is something you need?" he enquired.

"Nothing," Wayne started. "We came to tell you that my brother and I will be leaving this place today while there is a break in the snow."

"It is a good time to leave for the snow will not return for a few days." Ditan responded.

"We just want to thank you for the hospitality you have shown us for the past week." David added.

"There is no need to thank me but remember it so that if you meet a Sasquatch in the future, treat them in the same manner as we have treated you."

David and Wayne nodded, turned and left.

"What about you, are you also leaving?"

"Well, we were hired to track the Sasquatch by Susan." James answered.

"Which you did in a very capable manner! And now that you have done this?"

"To be honest after having seven days cooped up in an ice cave my only thoughts have been to get out and stretch my legs a little. We are employed by Susan and I am not sure if she wants us to stay so that we can lead her back home of if she intends to stay for an indefinite period. We will probably talk about this later."

"You are free to stay as our guests or leave when you are ready." Ditan said.

The boys thanked him for his generosity and left.

"What did you make of that then?" Matt asked as soon as they were out of earshot.

"My impression was that he meant exactly what he said. I didn't feel like there was anything that suggested that he couldn't be trusted."

"That makes two of us then."

"Let's go for a walk, clear our heads and talk about what we are going to do next," James suggested.

"I thought you said that it would be Susan who makes that decision for us."

"To be perfectly honest Matt I'm losing the plot as to who I can trust and who I can't. I trust David and Wayne but they're leaving. Weirdly, I find myself trusting Ditan, a Sasquatch I hardly know, but that's it."

"What about the others?"

"I've never really trusted Carson, I find him a bit of an enigma, Susan has shown herself to be a liar or at least a little deceitful. I know that she may have had good reasons to lie but... well, I just don't know. Sarah is Susan's friend as well as assistant, and this is only a guess, but she must know more than she lets on."

"Looks like we are on our own for now then. Let's keep everything we know or discover to ourselves until somebody earns our trust," Matt said decisively.

"I agree with that."

They walked for a while and returned just in time to shake hands with David and Wayne who had finished their preparations to leave. The Sasquatch were not to be seen, all in their caves sleeping.

Matt warned them to be careful of fissures on the plateau saying that he didn't fancy descending into the depths in search of one of them again. It brought a smile to their faces.

"Where are the others, aren't they coming out to see you off?" Matt asked.

"We've already said our goodbyes a while ago. They went off exploring like you did," Wayne answered.

"If you ever come to a little town called Wilson Creek, look us up. There will be a drink waiting with your names on it," David told them warmly.

Then the two turned and started towards the plateau.

They passed the rest of the day talking quietly by themselves, examining everything about their fellow group members, trying to get a read on them. By the time the sun had started to disappear behind the mountains and the light started to fade, the Sasquatch began to emerge from their caves and gather in small groups. This was behaviour that Matt and James had not witnessed before and they watched with interest. They observed that both males and females were gathering and so far they had not even spoken to a female member. Come to think of it they didn't even know how many of the Sasquatch could speak English.

Before long there were more than thirty adult Sasquatch in the gathering and just as the light lost its eternal battle with the ensuing darkness they watched as one by one the creatures leapt higher than anything in nature could leap and soared away from their home.

The boys went to check on and feed the horses since David and Wayne no longer had that responsibility. There were only two there. They seemed healthy and content enough despite the low temperature. Straw had been strewn over a confined area big enough for them to lay down if they wished. Then they went to the Susan's cave with the intention of finding out what they were expected to do next from her but she and the other two were not there. The fire burned brightly and had been attended to recently but even when they called out their names there was no response so they returned to their own cave.

"Where do you suppose they are?" James asked.

"Not a clue. Either they went for a walk or ride and haven't returned yet or perhaps they went hunting with the Sasquatch. I think the first because two of the horses were gone."

"Strange that! Two horses gone and yet there were three of them. I think they went off alone because I didn't see them when we watched the Sasquatch leave."

"No, but it was getting pretty dark and we could have missed them."

The boys prepared and ate a meal and as the evening passed slowly by it seemed more and more likely that Susan and the others had gone with the Sasquatch. They went to sleep unconcerned.

Just before dawn the Sasquatch returned home successful from the hunt. Ditan entered the boys cave and shook them roughly awake.

"Where are they?" The King asked.

"Who?" Matt asked drowsily.

"Where is Susan?"

"We have no idea Ditan; we haven't seen her."

"When did you last see her?"

"During the blizzard," Matt answered.

"What's this all about Ditan? We have only spoken to David and Wayne, who left yesterday, and yourself."

"Did they leave alone; you saw them go?"

"Yes, they left alone."

"Stay here, do not leave the cave." The King said before leaving.

Matt got up and went to the cave entrance only to find two large Sasquatch guarding it.

"I think our status has just changed from guest to prisoner," he told James.

"What the hec's going on?"

"I'm guessing that we are not going to find out until Ditan comes back."

It was an hour before the King returned and it was clear that he was still in an agitated state. He questioned them about the day trying to extract every little detail about it and Matt and James gave him all they could before, when answering a question for the third time, James held up his hand and said stop. For a moment the barrage of questions that he and Matt had faced ceased.

"We have told you all we can, three times! It's time you tell us what is going on."

"They have gone and we do not know how long they have been gone for. There is no sign of them anywhere and no tracks to follow. It is as if they have disappeared."

"Why are you so worried? We are free to stay or leave, that is what you told us."

"You are but Susan is not."

"You mean Susan is a prisoner here."

"No, we had an agreement."

"What agreement? We know nothing of this." James probed.

"It is an agreement between the Sasquatch and Susan of the humans."

"What is the agreement about?"

"It's about a meeting of two societies, yours and ours, about future relationships and cooperation."

"You are coming out of hiding?"

"It is possible, yes."

"Susan was the one who was making all this possible and Carson is recording everything to do with it."

"Yes."

"I understand why she is so important to you. Perhaps Matt and I could help find them."

"There is little you can do that we cannot. Our senses are better than yours."

"True but we can work during the day when you cannot and you can work through the night when we can't. We also think like humans which means that it is easier for us to work out what happened to them or where they might be."

"There are no tracks that we could find."

"The blizzard might have stopped but the wind is strong enough to cause drifting and cover their tracks."

"This is true. Where would you start?"

"The least obvious place is higher up the slopes so we can eliminate that direction. I think they would descend but they might not do it here if they wanted to hide their tracks."

Matt broke into the conversation. "Why Ditan, why would she suddenly leave? Is it not more likely that they went to explore and got lost?"

"I cannot answer that question. I do not know."

Ditan left the cave once more and the two guards followed him.

"Looks like we are free to go again. Do you trust Susan at all?" James asked his friend.

"I sort of do. I did, but now I am having doubts."

"Is that because Carson is with her?"

"I don't trust him."

"What about Sarah?"

"Although she must know about some of this I don't believe she is capable of doing anything bad. She is just an assistant."

Ditan returned. "It is agreed, you will search during daylight and I will during darkness."

"Right, it's light outside and we are wasting time. Matt and I should leave and start searching."

"Which way will you go?"

"We will go back the way we've come from."

"Why this route?"

"Everybody returns home eventually. It's what they know."

"We will meet with you tonight when the light goes. Find them, there is so much depending on this."

"We'll do our best."

"Wow James! I think we have just been employed by the Sasquatch…"

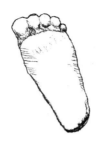

Chapter 16:
It's a Start

Matt and James wasted no time in readying themselves for the search. They packed enough equipment for an overnight stay, mounted their horses and headed off across the plateau. They heeded the warning about the number of crevasses on it and kept well to the left hand side where Ditan had told them there were fewer. The snow that had fallen during the blizzard was loose and deep in places and slowed their progress down significantly.

The four miles took over two hours to traverse before they started down the decline and both were relieved to be finally off the plateau. The slopes were no better, the loose snow treacherous, but from here they had the advantage of being able to see for miles. The two high forests they had passed through could be seen in the distance and James headed for the first of them.

"Do you think they are in there?" Matt broke the silence pointing to the forest.

"I doubt it. I think they'll travel for as long as their bodies allow them to. They'll want to get as much distance between them and the Sasquatch as they can."

"Why are you thinking like this James, it is possible that they went to explore and got stuck somewhere?"

"No they've left for a reason, they've hidden their trail for starters, somethings going on I'd bet money on it. Nothing makes sense at the moment except for the fact that the Sasquatch couldn't find any sign of them. That tells me that they don't want to be found. Look behind us Matt and see the trail that we've made. You could see it from a plane, it's so clear but the three of them have left nothing."

"You said about the wind moving the light snow and covering their trail."

"Our footprints are sinking in this loose snow as deep as some of the Sasquatch's that we tracked up the mountain. No! I think they have dragged something behind them to obliterate the footprints and the wind and loose snow would have covered the rest. That can only mean that they don't want to go back. The question is why."

"The only reasons I can think of for them leaving are: firstly for fear, do they have reason to fear their safety? Secondly, they might leave because they don't feel that this so called deal they have made is going to work out. Thirdly, they are leaving because they have something."

"What could they possibly have?"

"Proof James! Proof that Big Foot exists. The sort of proof that might make them famous and very rich."

"OK, let's assume that one of those reasons is the real one and examine each one a little more closely.

The fear thing, I didn't have any reason to suspect that we weren't safe or that we might be harmed. Even when Ditan was a little worked up this morning I never actually felt that we were threatened. As far as the deal goes, even if it was about to go pear-shaped, there was no need for them to leave without saying goodbye. Communication had already been started so even if one side or the other was not quite ready they would have wanted to keep the dialogue going for another time in the future.

"I like the sound of your final possibility. I mean, I don't really like it, but it does sound the most likely. Proof of Big Foot's existence wouldn't have to be anything huge, not if you are looking at something scientific like blood or fur. But why go now James? They had an option to stay longer, collect even more proof."

"Maybe they have enough already, who knows, but the one thing I'm sure about is that whatever the reason is, they want to get back unchecked by the Sasquatch."

"The woods would be easier to cover their tracks in than out here on the slopes."

"And also provide better hiding places for during the night when the Sasquatch are much more active."

"We know that the Sasquatch senses are more acute than ours but we don't know to what extent. I'm betting that Susan does and knows just how to use that information to her advantage. She'll know exactly how to conceal them from being found."

James passed some food over to Matt and suggested that they ate on the move rather than stopping. They ate in silence before Matt almost choked on his food as he spotted something in the snow ahead.

James raised his eyebrows in a questioning manner.

"Tracks James, tracks." He exclaimed dismounting and walking over towards them.

"Sorry to disappoint you Matt but these are David and Wayne's tracks, they obviously came through here yesterday."

"If we catch up with them it's possible that they have seen the others."

"I doubt it. The others must have left after they did because they were on their way to see Susan after telling us they were leaving."

"Not necessarily, we were the only two that saw David and Wayne off and they said that the others had gone exploring like we had."

"You're right, they could have gone before them. I'd bet that they would help us search if we did catch up with them."

"They would but in a place like this it's like looking for a needle in a haystack."

It was late afternoon when they entered the higher of the two forests and immediately the light diminished as the canopy above increased in density. They had less than two hours before it would be too dark to travel with any degree of safety. The darkness consumed the area around them, sooner than they expected, and they were forced to stop for the night. They made a fire and kept it burning brightly knowing that it would help the Sasquatch find them when they were about to continue the search.

The visit followed shortly, announced by the thudding of their feet landing between jumps. Ditan appeared before them and demanded to be told of their findings so far. He didn't hide his disappointment from them and James asked him if he could search the areas around the crevasses. Ditan understood the implications of what James was saying and nodded his acquiescence. Telling them that he would return in the morning to relate anything that the Sasquatch found during the night, he disappeared into the forest.

There was little the boys could do and they decided to retire early for the night. Matt banked the fire up so that they would have warmth when they woke and they moved into their tent. They lay for a while lost in their thoughts about this adventure and listening to the sounds of the forest before their attention was snapped back to the present. At first they didn't know what the sound was. It was distant, high pitched and somewhat eerie.

"Did you hear that James?"

"I did but I've no idea what it could be though."

The noise came again, louder, a little closer this time.

"It sounds like a human voice, a female voice." Matt said getting up and leaving the tent.

He was aware of James, who had followed him outside, beside him as he turned sideways offering his ear to the direction of the sound. It came again, this time much clearer.

"Hello, is there anybody out there?"

James did not wait for Matt to answer and instead just bellowed: "Over here."

Matt removed a couple of logs from the fire and, after passing one to James, started to wave his above his head. James followed his example before shouting out again telling the voice to look for the light. Silence took over for a while before a familiar voice yelled that she had seen the light. In the distance Matt and James could hear snapping sounds as Sarah trod on dry, brittle branches that littered the forest floor.

"I can see you, I'm coming," she called out and a minute later she burst out from the trees into the little clearing they'd used to set up camp.

"Oh thank goodness I found you, I thought I was on my own out here," she stated almost falling into Matt's arms.

James made her a hot drink while Matt attended to the cuts and scrapes she had on her face from walking into trees in the dark.

"Now that we have tended to your most urgent needs perhaps you can tell us what the hec has been going on, because we seem to have been left out of the loop, so to speak, and there are some Sasquatch who are not exactly pleased with the disappearance of their favourite human."

Chapter 17:
What is Going on?

"Susan made the decision to leave after negotiations with Ditan had reached a stalemate. She was insisting on him coming back with her and he, to put it simply, was not ready to do that."

"Were you present at the negotiations?"

"No, never! I was always told about them at a later point."

"What about Carson?" Matt persisted.

"He was present at a few of the discussions."

"Why did you all leave so secretly; why did you hide your trail and why didn't you tell me and James?"

"Susan believed that Ditan would prevent her from leaving. She said that she had told you already and that you had chosen to stay to study them."

"She never told us anything of the sort," Matt said indignantly.

James interrupted. "Why are you alone and wandering around aimlessly in the woods?"

116

"They left me. They told me that my services weren't needed anymore and they just left me. No supplies, no horse, no shelter. They left me to die."

Tears fell like rain down her cheeks and dripped to the forest floor.

"I can't believe what she did. I have worked for her for twelve years and it all comes to this."

She sobbed uncontrollably and Matt tried to console her with a hug.

James waited for the sobbing to cease before asking the key question.

"Do you know where they are right now?"

"I'm afraid not, I was dumped in the middle of nowhere. I decided that I would stand a better chance of surviving if I tried to return to the Sasquatch. I found the forest and was hoping that they would be around here. I was not expecting to see you here."

James filled her in on the details of what had happened after their disappearance and then asked about how Susan and Carson were travelling.

"They are using two of the small sleds behind the horses. Instead of riding the horses they are riding the sleds to save some of the horse's strength. They didn't think they had enough horse feed for the entire trip back. They are travelling fast though."

"How are they hiding their tracks?

"The sleds are trailing a bar with spikes, like a giant rake. The tracks are covered and the wind covers the shallow rake marks with loose snow. The tracks are hidden in seconds."

"Do these rakes have any other purpose?"

"Not that I know of, why?

"Sounds to me as if they were brought for just one purpose."

"Which means that this was planned beforehand!" Matt said whistling in surprise.

James suggested that Sarah went into the tent to get some rest saying that she had been through more than enough for one day. The boys stayed outside thinking about what they had just found out.

"I wasn't expecting this when we set out today." Matt muttered.

"I wasn't either. That poor woman, imagine being left out here like that, to die."

"It's cold and callous to say the least. I can imagine Carson doing something like this, especially if it was to save himself, but Susan?"

"They must have something very important to take back to resort to this type of thing."

"I think we will have to pick up the pace tomorrow if we are going to stand a chance of catching up with them. Perhaps we could ask Ditan to take Sarah back to the Sasquatch settlement when he returns in the morning."

"I don't think he is going to be too happy about all this," James muttered ruefully.

The boys did not sleep properly for the rest of the night, opting to doze by the warmth of the fire.

Ditan appeared just before dawn making no effort to arrive quietly. He was already talking before he crouched down opposite them, demanding to know if there had been any further developments. James told him about Sarah and Ditan made a sound like similar to a snort. They didn't know exactly what it meant but there was a tone of anger in his voice. He told them that they had been searching everywhere during the night, including the crevasse area but had not turned up a single clue that the humans had passed this way. Matt explained how Susan had been covering her tracks and the huge Sasquatch made the same snorting sound again.

"Tonight we will travel further down the slopes and search for them. It can only be a matter of time before we pick up their scent."

"How good is your sense of smell?" Matt asked.

"If they are out there and moving we will smell them from far away but we cannot smell their trail if it is covered in snow. We would see a light from a fire from a greater distance than a human too."

"Does Susan know this?"

"Yes, Why?"

"She is a clever person and she would know that she would have to conceal herself in such a way that your senses couldn't find her." James stated.

"We were going to ask you, if you could take Sarah back to your settlement, so she can feel safe."

"I'm going to stay with you and James. Thank you for your concern Matt but I intend to help you track them down." Sarah's voice came from within the tent.

A rustling followed and then the tent flap opened and she emerged.

"You are welcome to come with us Sarah." Ditan offered.

"They left me out there to die and I want to make sure that they are found and held accountable." Sarah said with a determined look on her face.

"We only have two horses Sarah." James stated.

"Well one of them will have to carry two of us, won't they?" Sarah stated emphatically and James knew that further pressure from him would prove pointless.

Ditan left with the same arrangements as before, to meet with them at sunset. They broke camp mounted and moved off.

The forest was very dense at its heart and the path they forged was anything but straight. Matt and James both knew they were losing time and probably falling further behind those they were trailing. They found David and Wayne's undisturbed footprints heading in the same direction as their own and knew that they were probably closer to catching them up than Susan and Carson. Every now

119

and then Sarah alerted the boys that she had passed by the route they travelled on her way to finding them last night. A fallen tree or a clearing were the features she remembered. It was taking far longer than expected to pass through and James wished they had travelled down on a parallel course to the forest.

At noon they dismounted to give the horses a rest and started a small fire to heat up some food and make coffee. They were travelling again within an hour although Matt walked alongside the horses to relieve it of some of its burden.

Again Sarah looked for places that she had passed and pushed ahead of James to ensure he didn't hide her view. Ahead she spotted her own set of footprints walking in the opposite direction and it became more apparent to the boys of just how far she had travelled on her own. She followed the footprints for a while before a rustling sound ahead caught her attention. It was immediately followed by a whooshing sound and a branch came sweeping toward her. It hit her high in the chest with sufficient force to send her backwards off the horse. She lay still on the floor as James dismounted and Matt came running over.

"Sarah, Sarah are you all right," Matt called out as he crouched and made to lift her head.

"Don't move her yet Matt, she could be injured and you could make it worse?"

Matt hesitated but ran his hands down her arms and legs to check for broken bones. He found nothing but before he could examine her further she opened her eyes and let out a moan.

"Where does it hurt Sarah," He asked gently.

"It's my head and my ankle," she moaned.

Matt ran his hands gently round her head. He found no signs of swelling or blood and guessed she had just hit the ground hard. He helped her sit up.

"If I am to check your ankle you're going to have to take off the furs."

She nodded and untied the belt at the waistline.

Matt averted his eyes as she started to remove them.

"Don't worry I am perfectly decent underneath," she said smiling.

With the furs removed she raised her leg onto Matt's leg.

"You'll have to remove the sock but be careful it's pretty painful."

Matt did as he asked and the started to move the foot at the ankle joint. Sarah moaned in pain.

"How is it Matt?" James asked with concern.

"There isn't any swelling yet, which is good but I suspect she has sprained it."

James searched for the small first aid kit packed away in their supplies. He found it and retrieved a bandage.

"Strap it securely Matt just in case. It shouldn't be too much of a problem while we are riding."

While Matt put his first aid skills to good use James examined the branch that had caused the accident.

"Look at this Matt it seems that Sarah is not a victim of chance. This was a trap that had been set deliberately to for us. Sarah's horse tripped the cord that held back the branch. Since it wasn't set to kill anyone I can only think it was set to slow us down, to allow the gap between us and them to grow ever bigger. The pace we have managed since we left the settlement has been anything but good enough, and since we know that they have already exited the forest they will be further away than ever."

"Don't worry James we'll catch them up, once we are out of here we will get quicker and don't forget that they have the bigger forest to get through yet." Sarah tried to alleviate his concerns.

"We might have to bypass the next forest at this rate." James muttered loud enough for Matt's ears only.

Two hours later they left the forest behind them and started down towards the next. From this height it looked very close but they knew from their original ascent that they wouldn't reach it before dark. Search though they did there was still no sign of a trail for them to follow. All they could do was keep going. Their quarry had to have passed this way, it was the only thing that made sense; out here there was nowhere else to go.

They made camp in a recess between some rocks just before dark; the wind had been getting stronger and was lifting the loose surface snow and creating a swirling mess around them. Ditan made his promised visit not long after a fire had been lit. He arrived looking even more agitated than he had been in the morning.

"You have some news for us Ditan?"

"I do James but it is not good. Mertia, daughter of my brother is missing. She did not return last night. She is one of the youngest Sasquatch at our settlement."

"How old is she?" Matt inquired.

"She is fifty-three of your years."

"How long exactly do you live for?" Matt asked. in amazement.

"I am the oldest in the group at two-hundred and seventy-four," the Sasquatch answered.

Matt's mouth opened in amazement but no sound came from it.

"How big is Mertia?" James took over.

"She is as tall as you are?"

"Is she just missing or was she taken?"

"She is a favourite of Susan's but there is no sign that she was forced against her will."

"Be decisive Ditan; was she was taken?"

"I think so, she would not leave her kin easily."

"Well Carson and Susan don't have her, I would know!" Sarah interrupted.

122

"If she has been taken then that only leaves David and Wayne then."

"I've never trusted them." Sarah burst out. "They never really mixed, resented working for us and were genuinely unpleasant."

"We know they are travelling this route Ditan, we've bisected their trail several times during the day."

"We will search for them tonight. If they have her the Sasquatch will not be considerate towards them."

"I understand how you feel Ditan but I am sure that they won't have her. There were only two sets of footprints and they were not made by a Sasquatch. Unless they were carrying her, they don't have her either." James pointed out.

"It is still possible that she has met with an unfortunate accident, a crevasse perhaps. We'll know more when we find David and Wayne," Matt added.

Ditan left with a morning visit planned and for the next two days no sign was found of Susan and Carson, David and Wayne or Mertia.

Chapter 18:

Rescue

They had already reached the second and largest of the high forests and true to their plan they decided to travel parallel to it to keep up the pace they had set. Ditan had kept up his morning and night visits but still found nothing significant to tell them. For the last two days nothing new had been discovered by James' group or the Sasquatch and things were getting a little tense as frustration and distrust set in.

Matt, James and Sarah sat around the camp fire drinking coffee while they waited for Ditan to arrive. It wasn't long before the ground started to shake and the coffee in their cups rippled in the same way as when a stone is thrown into a pool. Ditan's last jump finished on the opposite side of the camp fire. He landed so heavily that a shower of sparks flew up from the fire like a freshly lit sparkler.

"There has been a development during the night." Ditan stated with more than a little venom edged in his voice.

"What's happened?" Matt asked wanting good news.

"Another Sasquatch went missing. He was part of a group that were searching the furthest reach of this forest."

He hit the ground hard with his massive furred hand in frustration and another shower of sparks rose in the air from the fire.

"We didn't hear anything during the night. What do you think happened?"

"I think that whoever has Mertia has Bolvan too." Ditan let out an angry screech that rose the hairs on their necks and blocked out the hum of the wind.

"It doesn't make a lot of sense Ditan, one Sasquatch is hard enough to keep captured but two would be almost impossible even if the two groups have met up and joined forces." James almost whispered in an attempt to calm Ditan down.

"How big is Bolvan?" Matt asked.

"He is the third youngest; a little taller than Mertia."

"Sarah, does Susan have anything that could be used as restraints apart from rope, which we know they have?"

"Not that I know of."

"Look Ditan if they do have Bolvan then they are going to slow down significantly. The load on the horses is going to start showing soon and remember they don't have enough food to keep them much longer. Are you sure that there couldn't be another reason for Bolvan's disappearance?" James asked gently.

"It is rare that a Sasquatch has an accident but not impossible."

"Whereabouts was he last seen?"

"He was seen in the southernmost part of the forest a few hours before dawn."

"In that case we'll enter the forest here and travel the rest of the way through it, just in case."

"I am grateful."

"Before long someone will make a mistake and leave a sign that they passed by. I'm sure that they would have travelled through the forest. It gives them three days of cover. We have avoided the forest to gain time and we must now be a little closer to them. It is only a matter of time Ditan." Matt added.

Soon after Ditan left the small group alone, shocked and disappointed at what appeared to have happened.

"Right this is what we are going to do. We will enter the forest but not too deeply. I think that although they passed through it they would have kept to the edge to make sure they didn't get lost or go round in circles. The travelling would have been a little easier as the forest is not quite so dense there," James said decisively.

"Hang on a minute, I don't agree with you. They would have gone through the middle to avoid being found. There's more cover, more places to hide. Susan has a compass so direction wouldn't be a problem."

"You're wrong Matt I know it."

"You don't know anything more than I do, so you could be wrong."

"Look you know that I am the one for thinking before acting and you are the one who just gets stuck in. I should make the call. It's the way we've always worked."

"That was the case once but we agreed that we were changing, all the time we spend as adults is rubbing off on us. We think, act and even speak differently than we did before the start of the summer holiday."

"I agree Matt but I'm not wrong this time. We go through the forest close to the edge."

"No James, you go through the forest at the edge, I'm going through the centre."

"You're being very stubborn about this Matt."

"I could say the same about you."

"What about Sarah?"

"She can go with whoever she wants to."

James was feeling a little annoyed now but was not going to back down. Matt felt similarly.

"Ok! We'll split up for this part of the journey and meet up at the end of the forest. Agreed?"

"That's fine with me."

Nothing more was said as they broke camp and got ready to leave. Sarah decided to go with James after her previous experience, wandering around the other forest at night, had put her off going deeper into this one. They parted without a single word being spoken and for the first time since they had been time travelling together a rift had opened up between them. Each were aware of it but neither was prepared to concede to the other.

Matt continued on a diagonal course deep into the forest, long after James and Sarah had turned southwards. The course enabled him to continue forward, albeit at a slower pace, whilst looking for the centre. He muttered thoughts of frustration under his breath about James' stubbornness until he suddenly realised he was acting in exactly the same manner. He laughed at the realisation and hoped that James was thinking the same. When they met up at the end of the forest he knew that neither of them would apologise but also knew that neither of them needed to. It would be forgotten instantly and they would be as they had always been.

Knowing that he had two days travel left to get through the forest he picked up the pace. James and Sarah would finish half a day quicker. The forest was particularly dense here and he couldn't travel in a straight line which further slowed his progress. He ate lunch on the move but walked for a couple of hours to rest the horse. It was while he was walking that he heard a strange sound that didn't seem to merge with the other forest noises.

The sound wasn't human and it didn't remind him of any animal either. It came and went with random periods of silence between. He tied the horse to a tree and then stood still. He closed his eyes and concentrated hard on listening. Eventually it came again, a gurgling moaning sound, away to his right. He moved a few yards towards it before standing still again. Once more the sound came, closer this time, and yet there was absolutely nothing to be seen. He moved a few more yards. Again the sound, so close that he should have been able to see whatever was making it, but still he saw nothing. Still motionless he waited for it once more and when it came he knew that something didn't quite add up. It was so close it had to be hidden. He looked up and scanned the canopy. Nothing. He stared hard at all the trees that had trunks large enough to hide something, but no movement gave away its position. Then he called out. "Hello."

Less than three feet in front of him the ground moved. It undulated several times like a procession of waves and the gurgling moan sounded again. Matt took an involuntary step backwards before gathering his composure. He picked up a large branch that lay detached from its parent tree by a previous gale and poked at the moving ground. Something snagged it and when he pulled it back it the ground came with it. The more he tugged the heavier it got until it gave suddenly and he fell back on his bottom. He stood quickly and realised that he had uncovered a large and deep pit. His branch had snagged a net covered in forest debris to disguise it. He moved to the edge of the pit and looked inside. A Sasquatch lay at the bottom motionless apart from a hand that held a long branch it had used to move the netting above.

The creature's normally snow coloured fur was stained with dirt and patches of deep red blood. Three spikes protruded through the creature's body. One through a leg, one though an arm and one through the side of its neck. Matt was horrified. He knew that this trap had been made by humans and guessed that it had been made by the group he was following.

"Are you Bolvan?"

The creature made a gurgling sound as bubbles of blood coming from its mouth prevented it from speaking.

"Don't try to talk Bolvan, I'll get my first aid kit then I'm coming down to you."

Quickly, he fetched his kit which looked woefully inadequate to tackle the wounds of the injured Sasquatch. Nevertheless, he slid down the side of the pit making sure he avoided some of the other sharpened spikes at the bottom. There was absolutely no way he could move the creature or risk trying to pull out the stakes. Instead he bandaged the areas around them to stop the bleeding as much as possible. After attending the wounds he climbed out and lit a fire. It would be dark soon and he knew that the Sasquatch would come back to this area to continue their own search. He hoped they would pass close enough to see his fire and investigate. Then he slipped back into the pit and just sat with Bolvan.

The Sasquatch came three hours later, their keen eyes spotting the fire from far away. Ditan himself lifted Bolvan from the spikes that held him. Bolvan gurgled at the pain of it and his head slumped as he finally became free. Ditan lifted him up to waiting arms and he was carried away at speed back to their settlement.

"I hope he will be all right Ditan, there was little I could do for him."

"You did what you could Matt."

"This trap was made by humans, by those we are trying to find."

"It was made to kill Matt and that is unforgiveable; what is worse is that it was made by humans that we thought were our friends"

"I'm sorry we haven't been able to find them."

"They are hiding themselves well for we have not seen a sign of them either."

"We will keep looking."

"As will we."

Ditan left shortly after leaving Matt to contemplate everything that had happened. Despite having done everything he could of to help the unfortunate Bolvan he felt guilty. Guilty that a human being could do something like this to another creature. He didn't sleep easy that night

129

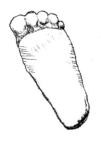

Chapter 19:
Capture

A day and half later Matt emerged from the forest and met up with James and Sarah who had been waiting patiently for him. Sarah had prepared a meal and coffee and he tucked in gratefully. Between mouthfuls he told them the details surrounding the unfortunate Bolvan. Both were disgusted by what they were told. Ditan had already informed them of Matt's heroics but hadn't given the level of detail that Matt did.

James and Sarah had nothing to tell Matt though. They hadn't found a single track and their disappointment increased when Matt told them that he hadn't either.

"It's like they've dropped off the face of the earth. I find it strange that we haven't seen any tracks belonging to David and Wayne for a while," James muttered in frustration.

"I think David and Wayne would have avoided the forest. Now that we know that they weren't involved in Bolvan's disappearance we also know that they had no need to seek cover and hide. I think they took the easy route and I think they are travelling fast," Matt responded.

"I'm glad that they had nothing to do with Bolvan. I was just starting to get to know them when they left. I was warming to them."

"Me too!"

"If they are travelling as fast as we think then they might catch up with Susan and Carson."

"I hope they don't; it could be dangerous bumping into two people you think you know but don't."

"I was thinking that we might continue travelling after dark tonight. There was a full moon last night that was easily bright enough to see by. What do you think Matt?"

"I think that makes sense, we must have made some time up on them. After all they must be wasting a lot of time in concealing themselves." Matt answered appreciating the concession James was making by letting him be involved in the decision making.

"Not just that, how long would it have taken to dig out a pit big enough for a Sasquatch?"

"I think it is too risky to travel at night; we could easily walk into another crevasse. We might even miss their tracks." Sarah spoke up.

"It's a risk we have to take and there has been precious little in the way of tracks so far." James answered.

Sarah gave a shrug of acceptance and Matt told her not to worry.

Two days later and with still no sign of their quarry they passed below the snowline. It felt good to walk on firm ground again. It was less than a day's walk now to the cabins and fresh supplies. That evening, just before dark, they approached the campsite. It was in darkness, no welcoming fire, nothing. Their belief in the fact that Susan and Carson would come back to this site had been total; there was nowhere else for them to go. The nearest town over twenty miles away. They couldn't hide their disappointment.

"Let's get a fire going in the cabins. Sarah I assume you are going to use the one that you and Susan had before. We will use the same one too. I'll get a fire going out here too and then tend to the horses." James suggested.

Matt grinned as James took on the leading role again without thinking. He didn't mind at all; his requests had been sensible and he agreed with what James had said. Perhaps this was how it was meant to be. It was fine as long as he approved of the suggestions but when he didn't he was going to speak up from now on. Even as he thought this James looked over with raised eyebrows as if seeking Matt's approval. He nodded a response. Later and with the tasks completed, Sarah made coffee and started to cook food.

Easy conversation took place while they ate but as soon as they had finished Matt brought up the fact that they had reached their journeys end without sighting the others or even finding a hint of a track. The question was what to do next, do they just give up or broaden the search towards the nearest town. They couldn't give up not while Mertia was still missing and they couldn't give up without facing Susan and Carson once more and demanding an explanation. Matt and James both felt they had to stay. The talking dried up, Sarah retired for the night and Matt and James sat around the fire lost in their thoughts.

James was far from convinced that Mertia's disappearance had nothing to do with Carson and Susan despite the fact that Sarah had told them that the Sasquatch wasn't with them. He wondered if something bad had happened to the creature that somehow Susan and Carson had been witness to. This might have explained their haste to leave. Perhaps the creature had met death in some way and they had hidden the body for later retrieval. The fame and fortune that might come from producing a Big Foot, even a dead one, was beyond imagination. There was always a chance that that the missing Sasquatch and the hurriedly leaving expedition members were completely unrelated. In which case did he and Matt really need to stay in this place any longer?

Matt's train of thoughts focused upon the point of their being there. In each of their previous adventures they had a major role to play and had become aware of their purpose at some point along the way. Their real presence here had yet to be revealed. It wasn't unusual to find it out toward the end of an adventure but this one seemed to have ended here with no explanation and no answers to their questions.

The two of them voiced their thoughts to each other but couldn't find any solutions.

"It's like one of those rugby matches where the score is low, there is nothing between the two teams and neither team can find a way to break down the opposition," James said.

"In that case do we accept the draw or do we keep looking for a way through?"

"We always play to win even if we are getting a thrashing from our opponents. In a game like that we try even harder."

"You're right James, that's exactly what we do and it's what we should do here. There is no way we can leave yet, so we need a plan of action."

"It's quite simple really, we need to keep doing what we've been doing for the past week, looking for tracks. Don't forget we excel at that, it's what we do."

"I've just realised something else James."

"What?"

"Ditan hasn't made a visit to us tonight, why do you think that is?"

"I wonder if we have got to the limits of his range or if he has found something that needs attending to. Don't forget there is also Bolvan, he was in a pretty sorry state when they took him back. I hope he hasn't got any worse."

Just as they were about to go to their cabin a sound in the forest caught both their attentions. The sound wasn't vocally made, it was more like something moving out there.

"Maybe it's Ditan." James suggested.

"It could be wolves." Matt countered.

They craned their ears for a further sound and waited. It came again, a rustling of foliage like something brushing it aside as they moved past.

"It came from that direction." Matt said pointing.

The noise came again, closer this time and James thought he saw a shadow move across his line of vision.

"Let's get a torch and investigate further." James said and went to the fire.

He returned to Matt and passed over a flaming branch. As they started forward they only managed three steps forward before a familiar voice called out.

"Stand exactly where you are and raise your hands if you value your lives."

Carson emerged from the forest with a Winchester rifle pointed toward their chests.

"What's going on Carson, why are you pointing that thing towards us?"

"I ask the questions here." He answered in a voice that conveyed a confidence that he had concealed before that moment.

"Where is Sarah?"

"You mean the girl you abandoned in the wilderness to die," James spat out angrily.

Carson laughed. "Yes that one."

James thought quickly and took a gamble that Carson didn't know that she was safely tucked up in bed asleep.

"She's safely with the Sasquatch."

"And where are the Sasquatch? I haven't seen them at all tonight; most unusual considering their recent searching for Susan and I."

James ignored the question and asked one of his own. "Where is Dr Blanchett?"

Carson moved as quickly as a striking cobra and James didn't have time to avoid the swing of the rifle butt hitting the side of his head. He fell to his knees as he reeled dizzily from the blow.

"I told you once that I ask the questions now; I have no intention of repeating myself," he laughed.

"You'll pay for that Carson, you'll pay for that several times over." Matt said with real venom as he helped James to his feet.

"I'm afraid that you two are no longer in charge but if you want to keep on like this Matt you can have a dose of the same medicine. Now move back to the fire."

James squeezed Matt's wrist to hold him back from doing or saying anything further and the two of them followed Carson's instructions. They stopped when they reached it but a prod from the rifle in Matt's back made him move forward again.

"Into the cabin," Carson barked and they entered. The door shut behind them and they heard the key turn in the lock.

"We're trapped James."

"What about the window?"

Matt pulled back the curtains. "It's all boarded up."

James slumped onto the bed and shut his eyes.

"You OK buddy?"

"A bad headache from the blow."

"Get some rest and I will come up with a plan to get us out of here."

Both boys were awake when they heard the key being turned in the lock the next morning. They stood back from the door as it opened expecting to see Carson with the Winchester. They could not hide their surprise when Susan walked in with a tray of food and some fresh coffee.

"I know! I know! You have a multitude of questions to ask me. There is no time now. Things are not as they seem and despite the fact that you have absolutely no reason to trust me I would ask that you do, especially if you want to come out of this alive."

With that said she turned and left locking the door behind them. The boys stared at each other open mouthed.

Matt voiced what they were both thinking. "What the hec is going on here? This adventure has more twists and turns than a country road."

"Are we to believe that Susan has no control over what has been happening or is she just acting a part to get us on side?" James aired.

"That's not all; why hasn't Ditan returned?"

"It's probably as well that he hasn't. If he sees Carson and Susan here, there's no telling what he would do to them."

"I wonder if Mertia has been found, that might explain the lack of visit."

"I still think that Ditan would want to see Susan again; they did seem to have reached an agreement that was important to both of them. That is, of course, if she was genuine and not part of whatever is going on."

Matt crouched down at the door and placed his eye to the keyhole.

"Can you see anything?" James asked him eagerly.

"Only Carson, he's sitting eating by the fire. There's no sign of anybody else."

"I wonder if Sarah's been found?"

"That's almost a definite yes because Susan would have found her in the cabin."

"If she is acting against her will then she may be keeping Sarah's presence a secret."

"Maybe there's hope for us yet."

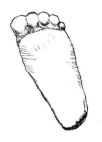

Chapter 20:

Escape

Susan brought them a meal later in the day too, but said absolutely nothing as Carson stood a few feet away, rifle poised. She placed it down and left immediately and Carson moved in to lock the door again. This time James watched them through the keyhole. Carson kept the rifle pointing at Susan and led her to the camp fire where she picked up a plate of food for herself. She moved towards her cabin, entered and Carson promptly locked her in too.

James reported the events to Matt whilst he continued to watch Carson.

"Looks like Susan might be innocent of the things we thought she was orchestrating. She is being held prisoner just like we are. I noticed that she only took one plate of food in with her so I'm guessing that Carson still doesn't know that Sarah is hidden inside."

"I don't think we should believe anything we see because this could all be fabricated for our benefit. I'm not going to trust anyone, not even Sarah," Matt said ruefully.

"Why would Carson still need to fabricate things? He has Susan, and he has us?"

"But does he have what he came here for. Does he have a Sasquatch?"

"If he had, would he still be here or would he be hightailing it to the nearest civilisation?"

"Whatever is going on I don't fancy our chances if we remain Carson's prisoners. We have to get out of here.

"You're right Matt. I have been looking at the door and the hinges are old and worn. There is quite a bit of play in them. We might be able to force the door away from the jamb enough to open it."

"We will have to wait for night time, when he's asleep. We will need something to use as a crowbar too. It will have to be strong enough to take a lot of pressure and thin enough to push in between the door and the jamb."

"How about a poker, will that do." He asked looking at the fire place.

"Perfect."

They took turns in watching Carson through the keyhole for the rest of the day and evening but the man remained fairly idle and night time seemed to take an eternity to arrive. When Carson finally retired to his cabin for the night, the boys waited and waited, making sure that he had time to fall deeper and deeper into sleep before they made their move. Finally, James said it was time to go and the pair of them moved to the door.

Matt took hold of the poker and inserted it just above the lock. He leant on it forcing it in as far as he could before starting to apply pressure against it. The gap increased but the locking bar still kept a grip in the jamb. James moved alongside his friend and applied his strength to the poker. The door moved away from the jamb a little more but still the bar held firm. They relaxed and the gap closed.

"We're so close Matt, if we repeat what we have just done but this time give it a sharp burst of extra pressure at the end I think it will give."

"It might make a noise James, the poker will lose its grip when the door gives and hit the jamb. It's going to seem very loud in the stillness of the night."

"It's a chance we have to take. Hopefully Carson is not a light sleeper."

"Come on, we're on the five yard line, one last push and it's a touchdown. We can do this James."

James grinned at the rugby reference. "I know we can."

They tried again and just when they were levering at maximum pressure they found enough strength to give it an additional sharp push. The locking bar slipped out of the recess in the jamb and the door swung open. The poker hit the jamb hard with a heavy thud and Matt and James held their breath as they watched Carson's cabin for a sign of a light coming on. No light came and they grinned with delight as they realised that they were no longer prisoners.

"What now?" Matt asked suddenly after realising that while they had planned their escape they hadn't thought what they were going to do once free.

"We have to rescue Susan and Sarah."

"I'm not so sure about that James. We can't trust Susan after everything that's happened."

"I know how you feel Matt but we can't leave Sarah. She hasn't done anything wrong that we know of."

"I doubt that we could rescue Sarah without waking Susan and if she is working with Carson then she would raise the alarm. We need to get as far away from here as we can."

"No James, I'm not going to help you rescue them, it's too risky. In fact the more I think about it the more we should be looking for Mertia. I think our presence here is about protecting the Sasquatch from those who want to exploit them for money and fame."

Matt was so emphatic that James paused to think about what he just said before answering.

"Ok Matt. I agree with you about our purpose, it makes sense. I can't agree with you about the women. This isn't a problem for the moment. Carson clearly wants Susan for something or he would have got rid of her and he hasn't discovered Sarah yet so that gives us some time. Let's leave and follow Carson's tracks. He has to have been somewhere before he surprised and captured us, so let's see where he's been. We'll give it twenty-four hours and then come back for the women. How does that sound?"

"Sounds good to me. Let's do it," Matt said. Pleased that his views had been listened to and making a silent vow to think before he acted impulsively the next time to repay his friends concession.

The boys pulled their cabin door almost closed and wedged in a piece of bark to stop it swinging open again. The locking bar prevented them closing it properly. From the camp fire position it looked like it was shut properly and James hoped that their absence would remain unnoticed until the next meal time. James lit two of the small oil lamps used around the campsite and passed one to Matt.

"Let's go," he said walking towards where Carson had appeared from the forest.

There was still at least four hours before dawn but the oil lamps gave off enough light to follow Carson's tracks. They were still following them as the first light appeared in the eastern sky. It was brightening by the second now and the oil lamps were put out. Just after that Matt saw something ahead.

"Is that what I think it is? He asked.

"If you are seeing another cabin then yes."

"Let's approach it cautiously just in case."

"Let's approach it from two sides, you go left and I'll go right. If there is anything suspicious going on, one of us will spot it."

"Get as close as you can without showing yourself. Even if there's nothing to see it might pay to just watch for a while in case someone's in the cabin."

They separated and headed off at right angles to the cabin before moving in for a closer look. There was absolutely nothing to be seen that suggested life at the cabin except for a mass of disturbed footprints that could have been there for some time. Both of them had taken up hiding positions behind some thick bushes and settled in to watch. Even if there was nothing here now Carson had been here during the last forty-eight hours. What they needed to know was why.

James waited for a quarter of an hour before deciding to move in. Just as he was about to signal Matt, a noise came from within the cabin. A dull thudding sound that repeated several times before stopping. James broke cover and ran up towards the front door. Matt followed his example and appeared at his friend's side. Three more thuds from within sounded louder this time. James reached for the handle and turned it slowly and quietly. He pushed at the door but it remained closed.

"It's locked!"

"Well it's either the owner or somebody who is being kept there against their will."

"Let's try the window."

They edged their way towards it being careful not to make a sound, but were disappointed when they found it boarded up. There was a gap between two of the planks but the space inside appeared blacked out.

"Enough of this stealth nonsense James let's just knock on the door."

James grinned. "Why not?"

They stood up and James rapped loudly on the door.

At first it was met with silence but when he knocked again the dull thuds returned, many of them in quick succession.

"Hello in the cabin, identify yourself," James called out.

More banging.

"I think whoever is in here is either hurt or a prisoner. We should break the door down," Matt suggested.

James nodded. "On three."

"One, two, three!" Both boys hit the door as hard as they could. It broke at the hinges and then into two as their momentum carried them inside. Their eyes acclimatised to the dark interior and they spotted a large, metal barred cage. Inside it, a Sasquatch lay down on the dirty floor, its fur stained red from blood in four different places. At an estimated six foot tall the Sasquatch was an obvious youngster.

"Are you Mertia, can you speak English?" James asked while Matt was already inspecting the locking mechanism.

A weakened nodded response came from the creature.

"Did Carson do this to you Mertia?"

Again the nodded response.

"You know who we are don't you Mertia? We are going to try and get you out of here."

"Looks like she's been shot at least four times Matt. She's lost a lot of blood and looks really weak."

"Carson's going to pay for this," Matt spat out in anger. The padlock on this cage is not going to break easily. We need something hard to hit it with."

"How about that axe?" James said pointing to the wall.

"That will do. Stand back James just in case something breaks off and hits you."

James moved backwards and Matt gave the heavy tool a full swing before bringing it down flush onto the padlock. It broke first time and James opened the door. He

142

examined the wounds on the creature before stating the obvious.

"Mertia needs a doctor."

"We haven't got a clue where to go for one of them but Sarah is good at first aid."

"We can't get her without facing Carson."

"If we don't face Carson then Mertia is going to die."

"Mertia is not going to die. What the hell is going on here?" A voice from behind them asked.

Matt and James turned in surprise to find David and Wayne standing just inside the door.

"Good to see you guys. We need your help and there's no time for explanations. Matt, you and David stay here and see what you can do to help Mertia. Wayne and I will go back for Sarah." He looked towards Matt to seek confirmation and Matt nodded. There was no time to waste and James was out the door almost immediately with Wayne following. David took off his backpack and rummaged inside for his medical supplies and Matt started to tell him about everything that had been happening since they had left the Sasquatch.

Chapter 21:
Face off

James told Wayne what had been happening as they travelled at almost jogging speed back to the campsite,

"We are going to need that rifle of yours to take him without a fight."

"Don't worry James, if necessary I'll have no problem shooting the man after everything he's done."

"That's too easy for a man like him; I want him to be punished for a long time."

"That will depend on if he comes quietly or puts up a fight. I think he'll make this difficult for us. He has too much to lose."

"When we came down the mountain we only found a few of your tracks. Why were you covering them?"

"To be honest David didn't like the amount of Sasquatch activity during the night. There was a time when we thought they were hunting us. I wasn't concerned at first but we saw Carson and the two women once travelling at speed. They were covering their tracks by dragging

144

something behind them. It made me think that David was right and that they were being hunted too. We copied their idea using a heavy branch to cover our tracks."

"But what about their other senses? We know that they rely on them too."

"We made snow caves to hide in at night and sealed the door. It blocks their sense of smell and as long as we were quiet they couldn't hear us either. They came very close several times."

"Ingenious, of course, that makes perfect sense. I wonder how Carson did it though; he had horses and sleds he couldn't have hidden them in the same way."

"If you ask me I would say that he outran them. They were travelling downhill. I don't think the Sasquatch would have expected him to have got so far each day and would have assumed that he was hiding up somewhere. They just didn't look far enough."

James nodded. "We haven't seen a Sasquatch for the last two days apart from Mertia. They seem to have stopped searching."

"Perhaps that has something to do with the other injured one."

"Possibly. Or are they just at the extreme end of their range."

"What do you mean?"

"Well the air is heavier down at this altitude perhaps they don't operate so well here. There is more forest too, good cover for hiding but not so convenient for travelling."

"There have been sightings in this forest in the past though, so they can come down this far."

"Looks like we have no definite reason for their absence at the moment then."

Their conversation had made the journey seem quicker than it really was and now they approached the campsite. They used every available inch of cover as they moved closer to the clearing. Carson was already siting at the camp fire putting more wood on and sending up a shower of sparks. He got up and moved towards the women's cabin and unlocked the door. He pushed it open and found Susan just at the entrance potentially blocking any effort he might have made to enter.

"He still doesn't know about Sarah," James said, "and he hasn't discovered that Matt and I have vanished either."

Carson moved to one side and allowed Susan to pass. She made her way to the fire and placed a pan on to heat. Then she busied herself preparing food.

"This is going to be interesting Wayne. When the food is cooked Susan will take some to give to me and Matt but we won't be there. He is not going to be a happy bunny?"

"A happy what?"

"He's not going to be very pleased and I can only guess as to what he'll do next." James said quickly covering up the fact that he'd used a modern saying before its time.

Twenty minutes later Susan took food to Matt and James' cabin. Carson followed, rifle poised. They hadn't even reached the door when he spotted that it wasn't shut. He pushed Susan to one side with a violent shove. The plates of food went flying and Susan fell to the ground. Carson kicked open the door and charged in like a raging bull. He came out looking flustered and angry. He grabbed Susan's arm and almost dragged her back to her cabin. He shoved her in and locked the door before doing a systematic search of the entire campsite.

"We have got to stop him before he gets to the girls' cabin and finds Sarah. I'll walk into camp and give myself up. I'll get him to turn away and then you can come in behind him and relieve him of his weapon."

"It's risky James; he might shoot you on sight."

"He looks pretty mad at the moment. He might rethink that when I tell him the entire campsite is surrounded by Sasquatch who will come in at the sound of a gunshot."

146

"You want to bluff him?"

"Only if I'm forced to. There's no time to waste, here I go."

James moved forward and entered the camp clearing.

"Looking for me Carson?" he said in a loud and confident voice.

Carson turned to face him and brought the weapon up pointing at James' chest.

"Put the rifle down Carson, this place is surrounded by Sasquatch. They will come in if you fire it. Can imagine what they would do to the man who took Mertia? Rip you to shreds I would think."

Carson looked a little confused at the confidence that James portrayed and cast his eyes around the edge of the campsite.

"You're bluffing, there's no Sasquatch in the woods here and what do you know about Mertia?"

"Mertia: six foot tall, female, shot four times and currently laying in a cabin two hours from here. She's not a prisoner anymore though and her parents are not amused at the way she's been treated."

Carson eyes flashed more than a little concern as he followed James who had been moving around him in a circular direction.

"Stand still," Carson snapped.

James complied but had already turned Carson away from the direction that Wayne would appear from.

"Isn't it about time you let Susan out of her cabin? We are in the middle of nowhere so she hardly has anywhere to escape to."

Carson took an intimidating step towards James and raised the rifle ready to strike it against the side of James' head.

"I told you the other night that I am in charge here. I make the decisions and you just keep your mouth shut and do what I say."

147

"You don't want to do that Carson." James said his eyes following the elevated position of the rifle.

"Don't tell me what to do," Carson screamed and then added, "Why not?"

"If you hit me with that rifle then the man behind you will shoot you."

Carson started to laugh, the maniacal laugh of a man on the edge of sanity.

His arm swung backwards but just as he was about to swing he felt pressure in the middle of his back. His eyes widened with surprise and he lowered his rifle before turning to face Wayne.

"You, how the hell did you get here?"

"Been here for a while now Carson."

"Let's tie him up Wayne; we'll secure him against that tree."

James fetched some rope and tied the man's feet and hands separately before tying him to the tree.

Wayne nodded his appreciation at James' skill with the ropes. James pulled the keys from Carson's belt.

"Time to let the women free I think." James said and marched over to their cabin. He unlocked the door and led them out.

They smiled a greeting at Wayne and gave Carson a look of disgust.

James told them about the unfortunate Mertia and Susan insisted on going to the injured Sasquatch immediately. It was decided that Wayne would take her on the horses while James sorted out a few things before following on foot with Sarah and Carson.

"What are we going to do next James?" Sarah asked.

"Food. We'll have some food and think about what we need to do next."

"That's so like a man to think of his stomach first," she said smiling.

"Always helps me think. I don't think there were any supplies at the other cabin so make sure there is enough to take some back for the others."

"There's plenty here."

They ate silently while James thought about their next move. He said nothing even after he finished.

"Not much of a conversationalist are you James?"

"There's a lot to consider and our safety could be at risk if we don't do things right."

"What do you mean?"

"Well can you imagine what the Sasquatch might do to some of us when they find out how injured Mertia is?"

"So what do you think we should do?"

"Still thinking about it. One thing's for sure there is safety in numbers and I think we should collect a few supplies and then go to the other cabin."

Sarah looked frustrated at the lack of any solid ideas but said nothing. She packed some supplies on a smaller travelling sled while James untied Carson from the tree and freed his feet. He left the hands tied behind his back and attached a length of rope to them. Then after attaching the sled ropes around his shoulders he ordered Carson to start moving. When the length of rope tied to Carson's became taut he moved forward himself. Sarah fell in alongside him.

"Make sure you don't get closer to Carson than the length of this rope. He's desperate now and desperate men are capable of doing horrible things."

Sarah nodded her response and then started to probe James for more information about what was going to happen next but he just told her that he wasn't quite sure yet. James set a good pace and they were soon at the cabin. The others greeted them and Susan explained that she had treated Mertia after removing two of the bullets which hadn't exited her body. The creature had been removed from the cage and lay on one of the two beds. David and Wayne placed Carson in the cage and locked the door telling him that it was time he found out what it was like to be a prisoner. He didn't go in without putting up a struggle though. Matt had a quiet conversation with James and left the cabin

Later as the group relaxed a little Susan explained what had happened at the Sasquatch settlement that led to the events that followed.

"Carson had met with Ditan to ask if he could leave to prepare for the historic event that I had been working towards. The meeting between the leaders of the western world and the Sasquatch. Carson had been told in emphatic terms that all arrangements were to be made by me and me alone. Knowing that he would receive little credit for all of this apart from recording the story, Carson stole all the evidence that proved beyond all doubt that the Sasquatch existed with a view to leaking it to the world bringing him the fame and fortune he desired.

"Unfortunately, he didn't understand all of the scientific evidence. He thought that fur samples and casts of footprint was enough. I had declined to tell him what else was needed so he decided to kidnap me and force me to tell him. When the kidnapping took place the unfortunate Sarah was in the wrong place at the wrong time and was taken as leverage against me to make me talk.

"Despite all Carson's attempts to conceal us from the Sasquatch he was discovered in the forest when he went back to for wood. On his return he boasted about killing a Sasquatch. I thought he was just bragging or saying it for effect, but shortly after he abandoned Sarah, we went back to the forest to get Mertia.

"I thought that I would never see Sarah again, and I did not expect to find Mertia still alive. I did what I could for her, which wasn't much. When we eventually got back here to the forest we didn't go back to the campsite, we came here instead. Mertia was dumped into the cage and then just left while we went to the original campsite. Left here for two days without food and water. Left here to die by a cold and callous murderer."

"Why was there a cage here Carson? You always knew there was a chance of catching a Sasquatch and this was your plan all along wasn't it?" David asked him with utter contempt in his voice.

"I planned ahead for all eventualities," Carson said and a smile erupted on his face.

"You're planning doesn't seem to be helping you now does it? James snapped.

"Oh but it does James. Take a look behind you and you'll see what I mean."

James didn't move but Susan's eyes widened with shock and compelled him to turn.

"Allow me to introduce you to my partner," Carson said.

James turned and found himself looking straight down the barrel of a rifle. Sarah stood holding it.

Chapter 22:
Bigger Problems

"I was wondering when you were going to show yourself for who you really are Sarah. I must say I am really disappointed that my suspicions have been confirmed," James said.

"There is no way that you could have known that Carson and I were partners," Sarah responded scornfully.

"Like I said, I had suspicions. If you think you are Carson's partner I would suggest you think again because there is no way that he is going to share the limelight with you when he gets back to civilisation."

"Carson loves me we are going to be married."

"Really! You believe that?"

"Never mind all that get me out of here." Carson interrupted angrily.

"What made you suspect me?" Sarah persisted ignoring Carson.

"Little things. Like when we found you in the high forest. You should have been worse the wear for your experience but you weren't. You tried once or twice to prevent us doing what we wanted to do, no doubt trying to slow us down, which of course was the reason for you coming back to us. Nothing concrete Sarah just suspicions that nagged at me."

"Sarah, get me out of here woman," Carson demanded.

"Let him out Wayne," Sarah ordered waving the rifle at him. Wayne did as he was asked.

"Why Sarah, why did you do all this? You had everything you could ever want working with me?" Susan asked sadly.

"Oh yes, I had everything all right, everything except a life of my own. There was no time for me to make friends or develop a social life, I was just your assistant, a nobody! Then you introduced me to Carson and he showed more interest in me during our first conversation than you have in the last ten years," Sarah responded.

"I had no idea you felt this way."

"You never asked how I felt about anything, it was always about you competing against the men in the science world."

Carson moved to Sarah's side and picked up David's rifle. He pointed it at the group and motioned for them to get into the cage. They had no option but to move inside and he promptly locked the cage door.

"Where is your partner James?"

"He's gone to fetch the Sasquatch, Carson."

"Yeah, yeah!" I'll ask you one last time James and if you don't answer with the truth I'm going to put a bullet through Mertia's brain."

"I've told you where he's gone; it's not my problem if you choose not to believe me. You would be very stupid to kill Mertia because she is worth so much more to you alive than dead."

"How so?"

"A dead Sasquatch means a few days of study before the body starts to decompose. But a live one... a live one

153

gives an opportunity to study more than just the creature's body. If you kill it because you don't like my answer then you aren't thinking long term are you?"

"There is going to be a moment soon James where I will silence you for ever," Carson said menacingly. "I am going to enjoy doing that a lot."

"Tell me about Bolvan Carson, when did you prepare that pit and the trap that knocked Sarah off the horse?"

"I didn't, both were already there, no doubt set by past Sasquatch hunters but it would have been remiss of me not to have used them against anybody or anything sent to track me."

"Sarah knew that spring trap was there. The strange thing about it was that there were no spikes attached to it. The trap was harmless and when Matt treated Sarah's injuries he couldn't really find evidence of them. Another thing that made me a little suspicious of her."

"Bravo. Bravo James. It's all rather unimportant now because we are here and you are in a cage."

"You won't get away with this Carson," David snarled at him.

"I already have and there's nothing that you and your brother can do about it either. I suggest that you make yourselves as comfortable as possible because your time in the living is down to just a few hours. Sadly, as far as the world is concerned, your lives were lost in a crevasse up in the mountains. The reality however is a bullet in the head for all of you and an unmarked grave in the forest."

With all that said Carson turned to Sarah and told her that they were going back to the camp site to get the horses and a wagon. The wagon was to be used for transporting Mertia.

No sooner had they gone than James was asked a barrage of questions about Matt's location.

He grinned and told them that all would be revealed shortly much to their frustration. They didn't have to wait long though before the cabin door opened and Matt entered.

"Anybody been missing me?" he asked grinning as he unlocked the cage door.

"Where have you been?" Susan asked.

"Outside, about ten yards away, hiding in a tree," Matt answered.

"But why?"

"James and I suspected that Sarah was involved and if our suspicions were true then it would only be a matter of time before she moved against us. I lay in wait for them to leave knowing that if they did then all of you would be in trouble."

"They've gone to get a wagon to transport Mertia."

"Which means that we have about four hours before they get back here."

"And what exactly are we going to do during those four hours?"

"We are going to get away from here and take Mertia with us."

"Just how are we going to move her, she is far too heavy to carry?"

"We have one of the small sleds here. I know it is too short for her to lay flat out on it but if she was placed in the foetal position she would just fit. She would have to be secured carefully though."

"Are you forgetting there is no snow here in the forest?"

"We don't need snow, the sled will work perfectly well on the forest floor."

"Where will we take her?"

"Back up the mountains."

"Carson will follow us for sure."

"He can't follow what he can't see. We'll hide our tracks just like David and Wayne did."

"We have a four hour start and with any luck we might stumble onto some searching Sasquatch and that should ensure that Mertia is safe from Carson's clutch."

"We credited Carson for some forward planning but I think you two should take a little bow for your own perceptions," Susan said giving them a radiant smile.

"Time for all that later once we get Mertia home," James said.

It took four of them to load Mertia on the sled, the unconscious creature unable to help in any way. Susan knew that it was touch and go as to if the Sasquatch would survive or not and hoped that moving her now would not exacerbate her injuries.

James and Matt set a fast pace, determined to put as much distance as possible between them and the inevitable pursuit from Carson. He would have horses, weapons and supplies to aid his search and subsequent capture of them. James and Matt had nothing of the kind and had an injured Sasquatch which would slow them down as they tired. They didn't lack the desire to try though and they knew that if they could get close to the snowline then there was always a chance that the Sasquatch would find them, assuming they were still searching for Mertia. James didn't think that Ditan was the type of leader that would give in easily.

Nobody complained about the pace but all had been quiet in their determination. After the four hours had passed James knew that Carson had now discovered that his former guests had been set free. He knew that the man would be in a terrible rage and hoped that his temper might blind him to rational thought. Somehow, even as he thought it, he doubted that it would make a difference. Carson had already proved that he was a very resourceful man. The decision to return Mertia was an obvious one and even if Carson didn't have a trail to follow he would know where to head. They would have to travel through the night to maintain any distance between them and he wondered if Carson would set off at running speed. If he did then they might get caught within the next couple of hours. It was starting to get dark already and surely even Carson would not risk injury to the horses after dark.

Patches of snow were becoming sporadic now and James really hoped the Sasquatch would venture down this far to search. Surely they hadn't given up; of course they hadn't given up. He reprimanded himself for having doubts. The snow became more persistent after another two hours of travelling and the sled moved along more smoothly. They were tiring and getting hungry but still they pressed on. No one complained and each had a determined look on their face. They had taken turns in pulling the sled Matt and James working together and then David and Wayne. Matt thought that they were made of the right material to play rugby alongside him. They showed no weakness and their desire to achieve their goal was admirable.

Another hour passed before a sound in the distance made them stop. They looked at each other and grinned. The screech carried down towards them again and they knew the Sasquatch were close. The sound gave them new hope and the realisation that, against all the odds, they might reach their goal before Carson caught them up. They moved faster now with renewed determination. The screech came again, closer this time, close enough for James to think about risking a yelled response. He hesitated, it was difficult to gauge exactly how close the Sasquatch were as sounds carried so easily on these slopes. It was difficult to know exactly how close Carson was too. He couldn't risk giving their position away too soon.

And then his dilemma didn't exist anymore as a familiar thudding started to approach them. James raised his hand to stop the others.

"They're here; we've made it," he said, not trying to hide the relief in his voice.

The ground started to vibrate beneath their feet at the impact of the Sasquatches' landings until they became so close that their own bodies shook too. An eight foot giant landed just in front of them. Then two more, and then two more. They said nothing but the first let out a screech so loud the neck hairs on each of the humans stood on end. Still nothing was said until another landed a few feet away with such force that Susan lost her balance and could not prevent herself from sitting down on the snow. Ditan stood before them, dwarfing his fellow Sasquatch, and making Susan appear the size of a garden gnome.

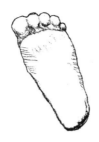

Chapter 23:
Trap

"It is good to see you Ditan and not a moment too soon," James started.

Ditan eyed him carefully before answering.

"You have Mertia with you. Is she still alive?"

"She is weak but alive. Susan has done what she could for her but she was shot four times. She had to operate to remove two of the bullets."

Susan pushed her way forward. "How is Bolvan?"

"Am I to just assume that you had nothing to do with all of this?"

"She didn't have anything to do with this Ditan I give you my word," James answered quickly.

"Ditan how is Bolvan?" Susan persisted.

"He is still of this world but he came really close to death."

"Is that why we haven't seen you these past days?"

"I was with him!"

"Bolvan's accident was freakish. The pit has been there for a long time; it didn't have anything to do with us."

"And Mertia, are you responsible for that?"

Susan nodded. "I'm afraid I am because I brought the man who is responsible for shooting her here."

"Where is this man?"

"He pursues us up the mountain. Apart from wanting to kill us he wants to take Mertia back to civilisation for study."

Ditan held back his head and let out the loudest screech any of them had heard. It seemed to go on for ever and by the time it stopped echoing around the mountainside their ears still seemed to be ringing from the effect of it.

Two of the Sasquatch picked up the sled carrying Mertia and left.

"Thank you for what you have done for her Susan but you know this is going to change our original plans don't you?"

"To be perfectly honest Ditan if Carson's reaction and ultimate greed is typical of what I am going to face then the world is not ready to greet the Sasquatch. Carson has no power in my world but he aspires towards it. There are those who have too much. I cannot, will not, expose your kind to unscrupulous people for exploitation."

Ditan sat down on the snow. "Tell me everything that happened from the moment you left our settlement."

Susan told the story from her perspective and James added details from the last time he saw Ditan.

"If we catch Carson and Sarah how will they be punished for their actions and what will prevent them returning with others to catch a Sasquatch?"

"No one will punish them Ditan because to my world you are still an unsolved mystery, a myth. Carson is persuasive enough to get others to come back here."

"And Sarah?"

"I think that Sarah has been emotionally poisoned by Carson. She thinks that he loves her and needs her help but I think he is just using her. That doesn't excuse her actions but

160

it does explain them. As far as I know she hasn't harmed a human or a Sasquatch."

"What about the rest of your group Susan?"

"They are not guilty of anything. We wouldn't be here now if it wasn't for Matt and James and David and Wayne; they have done nothing but support us from the start."

Ditan nodded accepting everything that Susan said.

"How far away are Carson and Sarah now?" Ditan asked.

"James?"

"They travel on horseback so no more than two hours and I suspect they are nearer an hour than two."

"We will catch them. They cannot return to your world and bring others here and they need to face the consequences of their actions," Ditan said emphatically.

"What will you do with them? Susan asked.

"I will make a ruling in two days after I have had sufficient time to think about what is best for all."

"They are armed with rifles Ditan and will not hesitate to use them if they are cornered," Matt warned.

"If they have no rifles then they cannot harm you. I think it's time Matt and I relieved them of their weapons."

"You have a plan James?"

"Yes! It involves a little work and we don't have a lot of time and we will need help from the Sasquatch."

"Tell us what you need and it will be done."

"Firstly, we need you to place a couple of Sasquatch on watch further down the mountain so that we have advanced warning of when they are near."

Ditan nodded to two Sasquatch and made a clicking sound. They rose and leapt away.

"Now the rest of us are going to build a camp with a fire. I want four sleeping places made around the fire and I want snow to be compressed and moulded into human shapes and placed under blankets to make it seem that we are asleep."

"Where are we going to be then James?" Wayne asked.

"We are going to be hiding in plain sight, very close and yet Carson and Sarah will not be able to see us."

"How does that work?"

"We are going to be hiding behind a bank of snow, which won't be snow at all; we'll be hiding behind the Sasquatch."

More Sasquatch joined them on the mountainside during the next quarter of an hour until there were twenty or more present. They adopted positions that made the camp look like it was nestling in a natural recess of banked snow. Standing next to them James could no longer discern them from the snow around. Their natural camouflage was perfect. David lit a camp fire while Susan and Wayne lay sleeping mats down and piled loose snow on top. They moulded the snow to form rough human shapes and then covered them with blankets. It wasn't finished a moment too soon as one of the Sasquatch on guard down the mountain returned to say that Carson was close and should by now be able to make out the glow of the fire. Matt added more wood to make sure.

It was time for the human members of the group to disappear from view. Ditan extended the skin, used for soaring, on his arms forming a shield big enough to hide Matt. His position was a few feet forward of the camp and Carson would have to pass by him to get there. All the others, except James, were similarly hidden to the side of the camp by other Sasquatch. The rest of the Sasquatch crouched and formed snow covered rock shapes and the trap was set. James sat patiently by the fire waiting for Carson to make his entrance.

It was ten minutes before Carson walked confidently into camp and pointed a rifle at James' chest. Sarah followed, also armed but not pointing her rifle at anything.

"Tell me James, in what world did you ever think you could out think me?"

"Lives were at stake Carson I had no choice but to try."

"Try and fail and now you will pay the ultimate price for that failure."

"I wouldn't be so confident if I were you Carson as you can see Mertia is no longer with us and without her you have nothing."

He had missed that at first, but now realised that Mertia wasn't there. He whispered something to Sarah who immediately raised and pointed her weapon at James too.

"Where is the creature James? Tell me or one of your friends dies and you know me well enough to know that I am not bluffing."

"There is no way I am going to let you take a Sasquatch back with you. Without us you will never find Mertia."

"Are you proposing a trade James?"

"No I wasn't!"

"Then I will. I will repeat my offer - tell me where the creature is or one of you dies."

James dropped his head. "Never," he muttered.

"Cover him Sarah, let him see what it's like to take me on and lose."

Sarah moved her rifle towards James and Carson took a step forward. He fired a shot into each of the pretend bodies.

James stared at him. "You are going to pay for that."

"Carson I didn't partner up with you to commit murder," Sarah said, totally shocked at what Carson had just done.

"Get over it Sarah, if you want to get anything in this world you have to be prepared to get your hands dirty."

"I thought you cared about me; what about all those promises you made to me?"

163

Carson laughed sarcastically at her before turning to face James again.

"Don't turn your back on me Carson, I don't deserve that."

"Of course you do Sarah. How could you possibly think that someone like me could be interested in someone like you?"

Carson still kept his focus on James and didn't respond further to Sarah's demand.

"I told you not to turn your back on me Carson." Sarah shouted out and tears flowed down her cheeks.

Carson turned to face her rifle pointing at him.

"Drop it Carson," she said sobbing.

"Or what? You going to shoot me? Don't make me laugh.

"She might and she might not, but I certainly will." Matt's voice took Carson by surprise, even more so when he felt the barrel of a rifle press against his back.

He was disorientated for a moment. Sarah pointing a weapon at his front and Matt doing the same from behind. He started to plead with Sarah saying that he only said what he did to fool James. For what, he never explained for as he brought his own rifle up, and despite the warning "Don't do it Carson," that Matt shouted, Sarah read his intentions and fired her rifle. Carson grunted as a bullet tore into his shoulder and out the other side. He dropped his weapon and Matt quickly picked it up.

Sarah kept hers firmly aimed at Carson until James moved forward and eased it from her.

Carson swore loudly at James who gave him a little smile.

"You only got the better of me because of this stupid little girl," he spat out.

"Wrong Carson! Take a look around you because all is not as it appears to be. The people you shot. Sadly for you it seems you missed because here they all are safe and

164

unharmed. I can see the confusion in your expression so let me help you understand. You shot snowmen and snowwomen." He pulled back the blankets to show him.

"Where did they come from?" Carson asked with less venom as he started to realise that he had been outsmarted.

"They were here, right in front of you all of the time. You just couldn't see them."

"How, How could they have been?"

"They were hiding under the protection of the Sasquatch."

Suddenly to Carson's shock, mounds of snow moved all around him as the Sasquatch slowly revealed themselves.

Ditan thrust his head forward so far that it trespassed into Carson's personal space.

"Remember me Carson. You are about to be a guest of mine once more."

Carson's body physically slumped as he realised he had been out manoeuvred and had no answer to his current situation. Sarah also stood with a slumped disposition.

"What do you intend to do with us James?"

"That is for Ditan to decide, after all, you tried to kill Mertia and that is a crime against the Sasquatch."

Ditan turned to James and the small group that stood with him.

"You will all come back to my settlement as my guests and witness the punishment we impose on Carson and Sarah."

They nodded their agreement.

"You have travelled long enough allow us to assist you in the journey to our home."

Before they could answer each of them were swept up by a Sasquatch and experienced the closest thing to flying for the second time in the past couple of weeks.

Chapter 24:
The Civilised World of
the Sasquatch

For the next two days Ditan kept himself remote from his human guests. Carson and Sarah had been kept in a separate cave from the others with two Sasquatch keeping a constant guard over them. Sarah had been ordered, by Ditan, to tend to Carson's wound since she had been the one to cause it. He wanted Carson fit enough to be punished. The rest of them had been free to come and go as they pleased and each of them found themselves inadvertently studying Sasquatch society and finding pleasure with what they witnessed.

"How much longer do you think Ditan will take before Carson stands trial?" Matt asked his friend.

"Somehow I don't think it will be much longer."

"You know this adventure is over. We were right in assuming that we were here to ensure the safety of the Sasquatch."

"I think we were here to highlight the fact that human society is not ready to share being at the top of the food chain with a creature they believe is little more than a wild animal."

"That makes sense to me but I wish the outcome had been different. We could learn a lot from them. We should be on our way home though and yet we are still here. It isn't necessary for us to see Carson getting punished."

"I thought that too, but you and me and David and Wayne, we are going back to civilisation and we take what we have seen with us."

"We aren't exactly going to share that with anyone."

"I know but if we did?"

"I see your point. What about Susan, you didn't include her?"

"I think she'll stay. The mission from her perspective has failed. She could take evidence back to prove the Sasquatch exist but for her it was more than that. It was about linking two societies. She feels guilty about what has happened. She brought Carson here and carries the burden of responsibility as leader of the expedition."

"She couldn't have known that Carson was going to turn out bad."

"I know, but he did. I think she'll stay here and record and write about Sasquatch life. One day her work will be published either during her lifetime or even after. Her study will contribute towards her original goal."

"That's assuming a lot isn't it James? She might revert to her plan of going to Africa."

"That was only an idea if her mission failed. In truth it hasn't, its only just starting, and I don't believe for one minute that she is going to give up."

"I hope you're right. So when are we going to go? I've had enough of all this snow now and we haven't seen the sun for ages either."

"We'll go after Carson receives his comeuppance."

They didn't have to wait much longer because Ditan announced a meeting scheduled for that evening. At last the end of the adventure was in sight.

"You don't think they have a death penalty for crimes like this do you?" Matt asked.

"I hope not, but if they did we'd have little say in it."

Later that evening they were summoned outside the cave. A huge fire burned brightly in a relatively flat area a little way from the ice caves. Ditan sat behind it, sitting tall with the rest of the Sasquatch semi-circling on either side of him. He indicated for the humans to sit opposite him but on the other side of the fire. Then he clicked vocally and a younger Sasquatch rose and left returning shortly with Carson and Sarah. The creature led them forward towards Ditan and told them to stand in front with their eyes lowered. Carson defied the instruction and glared angrily at Ditan.

"It is clear Carson that you hold little respect and value for Sasquatch life and the same can be said of your opinion for human life. This gathering has not been assembled to test your innocence or guilt because the truth is already known. You shot Mertia of the Sasquatch four times. One shot could have been claimed an accident but four shots announces that your intention was to kill. There were witnesses to this.

"The same disregard to life was also shown towards the humans here present. You willingly shot what you thought were sleeping members of Susan's group. People that were supposed to be your friends and fellow explorers. You did this all of this in the name of greed.

"Sarah your choice of actions to assist Carson were clouded by emotions and I have received a plea for leniency from Susan on your behalf. It is clear that Carson fooled you into supporting his actions but you had choices throughout your time here and you made poor decisions time and again. Whilst you never harmed a Sasquatch yourself, you

168

displayed little sympathy towards Mertia. You also did very little to help your group after they found you in the high forest. In truth you did as Carson wanted you to do which was delay them from finding him.

"Though your crimes are different, I have decided, as King of the Sasquatch, that you both will endure the same punishment. You will not be allowed to return to the world you came from. Instead you will remain here and serve at the pleasure of the Sasquatch. You will be treated well, far better than you deserve."

"And just how long do you think you are going to keep us here for?" Carson snapped.

"I thought I made it clear that you will never return to your people."

"And if I refuse to stay?"

"The consequences are serious. Without the assistance of the Sasquatch you will not survive. The place where you stand at present is not our permanent home. This is our winter dwelling. Our true home is higher in the mountains. The air is thin there and there is little food. The Sasquatch you would willingly kill without thought, will be responsible for keeping you alive. In time you will learn how to live alongside us, to be at one with us and your actions against us will be forgotten. This is the punishment that Ditan, King of the Sasquatch, casts upon you. How you react to this is up to you."

He clicked again and the two Sasquatch that brought the prisoners to him led them away. Sarah said nothing as she walked away but Carson's head slumped as he recognised there was nothing he could do to escape this. He too said nothing.

Ditan turned to his other guests. "It is time for you to decide if you wish to stay or leave. The Sasquatch will welcome you if you stay and remember you if you leave. What is it that you wish?"

Wayne and David told him that they wished to return home and after a few words of thanks from Ditan, two Sasquatch moved forward. Each lifted one of the brothers and leapt from the settlement.

"They will be at the campsite below the snowline before morning," Ditan announced. What about you Susan do you wish to leave or stay?"

"We started something that has yet to be finished Ditan. Despite all that has happened, I would like to stay and continue our work towards a meeting of our peoples."

"Your choice pleases me. Matt and James what are your intentions?"

"We need to leave Ditan, there are more adventures waiting for us and we can't resist an adventure," James answered.

"Then go with the thanks of the Sasquatch and know that you have friends here whenever you need them."

He clicked and two Sasquatch plucked them up and they found themselves soaring down the mountain slopes.

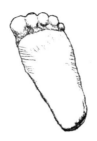

Chapter 25:
Homeward Bound

They arrived at the campsite sometime after David and Wayne who had already left for home. There was not much point in them remaining here for any amount of time either so, after expressing their thanks to the two Sasquatch, they started the long walk back towards the waterfall. They broke into idle chatter about the adventure they had just experienced.

"I have to say I never believed in the existence of the Sasquatch," Matt said breaking the silence of the last half an hour.

"Me neither, but it's like the Loch Ness Monster thing. Both myths were equally strongly supported and doubted. If I've learned anything here then it's not to be close-minded about myths."

"I wonder how Carson is going to get on living with creatures he has no time for."

"He's lucky. In the 1920's the death penalty was still used and he might well have received that had he faced charges in his own society."

"Do you think they will treat him well?"

"Yes, and in time I think he might even reform a little."

"Hope so!"

"This adventure had a lot of twists and turns which led us to believe that Susan was a villain when she wasn't."

"I know, we jumped to conclusions a bit. But to be fair to us, the evidence at the time was stacked against her. It's not the first time we've read something wrong and it probably won't be the last. Hopefully we will get better at being less judgemental until we are absolutely, beyond all doubt, sure."

"Some of the situations we got into gave us problems too. We argued and separated at one stage."

"We are different Matt and we are going to have different opinions now and again. I think its ok. If you hadn't gone your own way here then Bolvan wouldn't have survived the pit. You saved him Matt."

"I suppose so, but it seems strange for us to argue, we never do outside one of these adventures."

"I think that's because we take on a little more than just an adult body when we go through the portal."

"What do you mean?"

"Think about it for a moment. We talk differently, have different skills so it stands to reason that we might think a little differently too."

"You're probably right."

They fell silent for a while as each thought about their roles and how different they had been to their normal selves. James, in particular, reflected on how both he and Matt changed a little during an adventure and brought something extra back to their own time when they returned. It wasn't just the skills they had used there but it was like they had returned with a tiny essence of the character they had been. It happened every time they came back and little by little it was changing the way they acted and thought. Some

172

would say that as teenagers they were just maturing naturally, but they were experiencing things far in excess of what a normal teenager would go through. James thought the changes were for the better as far as he and Matt were individually concerned but he worried a little for them both as a team.

Their thoughts took their minds away from the long trek back and before long they were standing in front of the waterfall once more.

"You know what I am going to do first when I get back James?"

"Knowing you like I do, I would guess that food plays a part."

Matt laughed. "I've had enough of that stew to last me the next ten years. What I really fancy, like right now is some egg and bacon with a hunk of fresh bread."

They passed through the waterfall and entered the cave before James answered his friend.

"I could manage a meal like that. My house or yours?"

"You got ketchup?"

"Course!"

"Yours then."

'The Walking With Series'

by C. S. Clifford:

For the 8 – 13 age group:

Walking with the Hood

ISBN: 9780993195730

'The Walking With Series'
by C. S. Clifford:
For the 8 – 13 age group:

Walking with Nessie

ISBN: 9780993195709

'The Walking With Series'

by C. S. Clifford:

For the 8 – 13 age group:

Walking with the Fishermen

ISBN: 9780993195723

'The Walking With Series'
by C. S. Clifford:
For the 8 – 13 age group:

Walking with the Magician

ISBN: 978099319577

C. S. Clifford has always been passionate about stories and storytelling. As a child he earned money singing at weddings in the church choir; the proceeds of which were spent in the local bookshop.

As a former primary teacher, he was inspired to start writing through the constant requests of the children he taught. He lives in Kent where, when not writing or promoting and teaching writing, he enjoys carpentry, sea and freshwater angling and exploring the history of his local countryside.